One Hot CHANCE

Hot Brits, Book One

ANNA DURAND

JACOBSVILLE BOOKS JB MARIETTA, OHIO`

ONE HOT CHANCE

ISBN: 978-1-949406-22-1 (paperback)
ISBN: 978-1-949406-23-8 (audiobook)

Manufactured in the United States.

Jacobsville Books
www.JacobsvilleBooks.com

Publisher's Cataloging-in-Publication Data
provided by Five Rainbows Cataloging Services

Names: Durand, Anna.
Title: One hot chance / Anna Durand.
Description: Marietta, OH : Jacobsville Books, 2020. | Series: Hot Brits, bk. 1.
Identifiers: ISBN 978-1-949406-22-1 (paperback) | ISBN 978-1-949406-23-8 (audiobook)
Subjects: LCSH: Legal assistants--Fiction. | Attorneys--Fiction. | Man-woman relationships--Fiction. | British--Fiction. | New York (N.Y.)--Fiction. | Romance fiction. | BISAC: FICTION / Romance / Contemporary. | FICTION / Romance / Romantic Comedy. | FICTION / Romance / Workplace. | GSAFD: Love stories.
Classification: LCC PS3604.U724 O54 2020 (print) | LCC PS3604.U724 (ebook) | DDC 813/.6--dc23.

Praise for Anna Durand's Books

"[*Lethal in a Kilt* is] full of hot sex, adventure, and so much laughter. I found myself laughing-out-loud at the antics of the Witches of Ballachulish (Logan's sisters) and the hilarious flirting and sexy banter between Serena and Logan. [...] Recommend highly! "
Sharon Clayton, The Eclectic Review

"[*Insatiable in a Kilt*] smokes from the very first pages... Durand's characters are a delight and seeing how they mix business with their increasing attraction for each other is entertaining indeed. [...] Durand's Hot Scots family saga just keeps on getting better."
Readers' Favorite

"[*Notorious in a Kilt*] is the book I have been waiting for! A great second-chance romance and one of my favorites in this series."
The Romance Reviews

"I loved the Scottish in Ian and the strength of Rae, but the love of one little girl makes [*Notorious in a Kilt*] something to behold."
Coffee Time Romance

"*Gift-Wrapped in a Kilt* is a marvelous continuation of the author's MacTaggart family saga. Durand's story has an entertaining plot, and her steamy interludes are well-written...a celebration of healthy relationships between loving adults written in a tasteful and compelling manner."
Readers' Favorite

"I have enjoyed this whole series, but Emery and Rory [from *Scandalous in a Kilt*] have stolen my heart and are now my favorites!"
The Romance Reviews

"An enthralling story. [...] I highly recommend the writing of Ms. Durand and *Wicked in a Kilt*, but be warned you will find yourself addicted and want your own Hot Scot."
Coffee Time Romance & More

"There's a huge hero's and heroine's journey [in *Dangerous in a Kilt*] that I quite enjoyed, not to mention the hot sex, and again, not to mention the sweet seduction of the Scotsman who pulls out all the stops to get Erica to love him."
Manic Readers

Other Books by Anna Durand

Chapter One

Elena

I am cursed. Seriously. Since I was born on the thirteenth day of October—Friday the thirteenth, no less—I feel justified in declaring myself to be cursed. Why else would I get my dream job only to discover it's a nightmare? I've admired Raisa Volkov for years and followed her legal career like a true fangirl. Becoming her paralegal seemed like an awesome gift. I get to work alongside the toughest, most successful divorce attorney in New York.

Except she's hated me from day one. She snips at me, snaps at me, barks orders at me, and generally makes me wish I'd taken a job at McDonald's instead. I suppose I should be comforted by the fact she makes everyone feel that way, but it doesn't comfort me at all.

And this is only day two. Thank God it's Friday.

Now I understand why Raisa's former paralegal, Mia, gave her two-week notice sixteen days ago. Her Royal Snippiness tasked Mia with hiring her own replacement.

That would be me. The cursed Elena Linwood.

While I fantasize about murdering my new boss, I raise a hand to get the bartender's attention. I just sat down at the bar a minute ago and desperately need booze. I mean *desperately*. Two days with Raisa have left me drained and depressed. So here I sit, in the swanky hotel across the street from the office, on a Friday night, about to drown my sorrows in a margarita. The bartender takes my order, smiling and calling me "babe," though not in a creepy way. He's cute and sexy, but way too busy to flirt with me. "Sure thing, babe" is all I get out of him.

God, I need a hot guy to flirt with. To dance with. To do all sorts of naughty, naughty things with.

That proverbial light bulb goes off in my head. A bright, flashing, neon-pink bulb. What do I need to lift my spirits? Why, a steamy fling with an anonymous piece of sizzling-hot ass.

You're brilliant, Elena.

I congratulate myself on my awesome idea for about thirty seconds. Then reality slams down on my head as I glance around the bar. It's full of older couples and middle-aged men on their own who look like they probably just got served divorce papers and want to get hammered. I have a feeling a lot of men who get served by Raisa Volkov wind up in this bar after their first meeting with their wives' attorney.

No hot prospects. Looking at these guys makes me want to face-plant on the bar.

So I do. And I moan, like the pathetic wage slave I am.

"You still want the drink?" the bartender asks.

I don't bother to raise my head, instead waving my hand to indicate that yes, I do want that margarita. I plan to guzzle it like a sorority girl at a frat party. As soon as I can peel my face away from the shiny, cool surface of the bar. I hear the cute bartender set my drink down.

Maybe I should've ordered straight-up tequila.

"Are you all right there?"

That voice. It's not the cute bartender. The man who spoke to me has a silky British accent and a husky voice that makes me want to crawl onto his lap without even looking at his face. Since I am cursed, I know if I do look, I'll find out he has the face of a bulldog and the body of a sumo wrestler.

But that voice…

A warm hand touches my arm. Since I'm wearing a sleeveless blouse, I get to feel his skin on mine. Oh, it feels sooo good.

"I said are you all right?" he asks.

"Mm-hm." I finally peel my face away from the bar—and sit up straighter. Blue eyes. Blond hair. A body to die for. *Lucky me.* Everything south of my waist wakes up from its months-long coma and tingles in all the right ways when he smiles at me. I smile back. "I'm fine, but thanks for asking. I love polite British men."

Why did I say that? *Stupid, stupid Elena.*

He lifts one brow and smirks. "How do you know I'm polite? I've barely spoken five words to you."

"Seven, actually. Unless you count the ones you said twice, which would mean eleven words. Not including what you said a second ago."

Oh. My. God. Why do stupid things keep pouring out of my mouth? It's not like I've never seen a hot guy before.

He leans against the bar, his beautiful blue eyes twinkling in the subdued lighting. "It's comforting to know you're intelligent enough to count to at least eleven."

"I can count to twelve in German."

"Can you?" He's still smirking, but damn, that expression makes me start to tingle above the waist too. His voice gets even deeper, even sexier, when he says, "Let me hear it."

What the hell. I slant toward him a little, enough that I can smell his spicy cologne, or maybe it's aftershave. Either way, the scent makes me want to lick him from head to toe. "*Eins, zwei, drei, vier, fünf, sechs, sieben, acht, neun, zehn, elf, zwölf.*"

"Say *zwölf* again. I love the way you pronounce it."

He loves my pronunciation? I really hope he isn't making fun of me.

The sexy Brit leans in to brush hair away from my face, his fingers grazing my skin. "Say it again, please."

I grin. "See, you are polite."

"For the moment." He trails his fingertips down my cheek to the corner of my mouth. "Say *zwölf* again, and I'll kiss you."

"What if I don't want to kiss you?"

He drags one finger across my mouth, slowly, sensuously. "You do."

Yeah, okay, I do. My fling idea sounds better and better every second.

I lick his finger and say, "*Zwölf.*"

He slides his hand into my hair, pulls my face closer, and kisses me.

Oh God, his lips. They're soft and warm, and taste faintly of caramel. Maybe he had a decadent dessert a few minutes ago. I don't care, because all I want is for his lips to tease mine for the rest of eternity. His breaths tickle my skin, and my nipples go hard. When he slips his tongue between my lips, I melt. I'm floating on a warm, silken cloud of desire, my body pure liquid and the only thing keeping me from collapsing into a puddle at his feet is his mouth.

He pulls away, but only a few inches. "Come to my room with me."

"What?" Sure, it's exactly what I wanted, but my brain can't quite catch up to his words.

"Come with me, upstairs, to my room." He catches my bottom lip with his teeth, swipes his tongue over it, and releases my flesh with a slowness that makes me ache in all the best ways. "You're the most adorable creature I've ever seen, and I want to make love to you all night long."

"Oh God, yes." Did I say that out loud? *Ugh, Elena, stop doing that.* "Let's go to your room."

"Do you want to finish your drink first?"

I glance sideways at the untouched margarita. Suddenly, my scorching Brit sounds like a much better cocktail than the drink I ordered. "No, I'm done with it."

He slings an arm around my waist as I ooze off my stool, slinging my too-big purse over my shoulder. We walk across the lobby to the elevator with me hugged to his hard body and his hand on my hip.

The elevator doors open. Three people hurry out, leaving the car empty.

My Brit and I get in, and the doors glide shut.

He turns toward me, still hugging me to him, and I suddenly find myself plastered to the hottest body I've ever seen—and the stiffest hard-on I've ever felt.

"Can't wait," he almost growls. "I'm on the nineteenth floor, which means we have time."

"Time for what?"

He backs me up to the wall and crushes his mouth to mine. His tongue thrusts deep, making me moan and latch my arms around his neck. I'm helpless to resist his hungry swipes, helpless to do anything except let him ravage me and mash me to the wall with every inch of his delicious body. I moan again, rougher, needier.

And he shoves my skirt up.

I gasp, but then grin like an idiot. My purse slides off my shoulder, thumping on the floor.

He tears my panties off, his expression tight with need and a craving so intense it seems to bleed into me, making me slicker and hotter and achier. He unzips his slacks while he seals his mouth over my nipple, soaking my blouse and bra, and suckles the tip. My back arches. I clutch his head to my chest, loving the softness of his hair and the sharp sting of his teeth scraping my hard peak.

I barely notice when the sound of foil ripping fills the elevator.

My Brit pulls away only long enough to sheath himself with a condom, then he hoists one of my legs and thrusts into me.

A cry bursts out of me, surprise and lust and sheer ecstasy rushing through me like high tide on a full moon night.

He pushes inside me again and again, every thrust strong and purposeful, his cock penetrating me so deeply it's like our bodies were made for each other. He consumes me, unrelenting in his passion, and soon his movements grow wilder, greedier, like he can't get enough of me and never wants this to end. I want it to go on and on and on. The slapping of our bodies as they collide becomes a frantic rhythm, while I bounce and he grunts every time he slams me into the wall.

I come like a fireworks display on New Year's Eve, every burst of pleasure bigger and hotter and brighter, blinding me to everything except the look on his face. No man has ever looked at me that way, like he can't bear to give up being inside me but can't wait a second longer to let go.

His climax pulsates deep inside me, and I come harder.

We both go limp. I sag against the wall. Luckily, he has enough strength left to keep us both from falling into a lump on the floor. He nuzzles my neck, then peppers soft kisses on my skin as he makes his way up to my ear.

A phone rings.

Not mine.

My Brit digs his phone out of his pocket and answers it. "What do you want?"

He sounds irritated.

I'm kind of irritated too. I mean, he's still inside me, and he takes a call? What the hell? So much for politeness.

"I'm busy," he says curtly, his mouth pinched. "We can talk about this Monday."

While he chats with somebody else, I wriggle away from him, fix my dress, and stuff my wrecked panties into my purse.

The elevator stops. The doors open.

I don't have a room on the nineteenth floor, or anywhere in this hotel, but I suddenly need to get away from him. My plan to cheer myself up with a fling started out so hot, but now I'm feeling weird about the whole thing. So I stumble out into the hall.

"Wait," he calls out to me.

I turn toward him, hoping my expression conveys how much I don't like being screwed and then forgotten about.

He's holding his phone to his chest and giving me the sweetest look of regret. "Please wait. I'm sorry about this."

Being a total sucker for a pitiful, hot man—not to mention a sucker for a British accent—I chew my lip and try to decide what to do. I can hear the person he's been talking to shouting at him, demanding his attention.

"Not now," he hisses into the phone.

I hear more tinny shouting. My shoulders sag, because obviously, this is the end of my hot night of sin with a stranger. Like I said, I'm cursed. I get one good bang in an elevator, and then it's over.

He looks at me again, his expression pleading for me to stay.

I shake my head and march toward the stairs. I do my dramatic exit thing, then schlep down one flight of stairs before I realize I can't walk down eighteen more flights. Groaning at my sucky luck, I sit down on the steps and face-plant in my own hands this time.

The clapping of shoes echoes in the stairwell, coming down the steps from the floor above.

Someone sighs right beside me.

I peek through my fingers at the person.

My sexy Brit is kneeling beside me, looking a little embarrassed. "I'm sorry about that. I shouldn't have answered my phone."

A shrug is all I can manage in response. I'm still covering my face with my hands and watching through the gaps between my fingers.

He gently pries my hands away, clasping them in his bigger ones. "Please come to my room. I'd love to spend all night with you. You're the most enchanting woman I've ever met."

Enchanting? No one has ever called me that before. He'd also said I'm adorable. He is definitely adorable, enchanting, sexy, beautiful, and all sorts of other adjectives.

I open my mouth to accept his offer when my phone chimes, alerting me to a new text. Since I got annoyed when my Brit took a call, I can't check my text. I clutch my purse to my stomach, chewing on my lip.

"You can check that," he says. "It's all right."

"Sorry," I say as I pull out my phone and read the text.

It's from my brother, Kyle. He says, "Where R U?"

Oh crap. I forgot I'm supposed to spend the evening with him, hanging out, before he and his girlfriend leave for their spring break vacation tomorrow morning.

"You need to go," my Brit says.

Wincing, I say, "Yeah. It's, um, a family thing I forgot about."

"May I know your name?"

"Elena." I get an idea, and rummage in my purse until I find an old Starbucks receipt and a pen. I scribble numbers on the back, then hand the paper to him. "Here's my number."

He smiles. "Thank you, Elena. I'm Chance, by the way."

The man I just had sex with is called Chance. Maybe my luck is changing. I try not to read too much into his name, since chance is a roll of the dice, not a good omen.

We both get up.

He kisses my cheek. "I'll ring you tomorrow, if that's all right."

"Yes, I'd like that."

I allow myself one last look at his blue eyes, then I walk out of the stairwell and take the elevator to the lobby. When I get home, Kyle is waiting for me with two pizzas and a six-pack of beer. We have fun watching action movies until two o'clock, but when I fall asleep, I dream of the sexy Brit.

Will he call me?

As it turns out, no. My luck hasn't changed at all.

Chapter Two

Elena

I arrive at the offices of Raisa Volkov & Associates on Monday morning feeling surprisingly good, despite having spent the weekend at the office working overtime without the overtime pay. This is the life of a paralegal. I no longer feel like a loser who had a quickie in an elevator and never got a callback. Definitely not like the girl who had face-planted on the bar, or the girl who counted to twelve in German. No, I'd left that idiot behind. Locked her in the hotel basement, actually.

Still, my sexy Brit had liked the silly things I'd said. At least, he seemed to like them. Maybe he was pretending to, so I'd have sex with him. Whatever. I'd wanted a fling, and I'd had one. Yay, me.

I sit down at my desk in the cubicle zone and resolve to never think of Friday night again. My large, steaming latte from Starbucks calls to me, so I take a swig. Mm, yummy goodness.

A memory of the sexy Brit's face pops into my mind. Oh yeah, yummy goodness there.

Stop that, I command myself. *You're a strong, capable woman who has a freaking job to do.*

Yes, I do. My job sucks in every way imaginable, but I will do it anyway. Straightening in my chair, I take another sip of my latte and log on to my computer. Like the other paralegals and the interns, I have a crummy chair inside a crummy cubicle. My coworkers named all of us the plebs, a term taken from ancient Rome, which means we're the dirt Empress Raisa scrapes off her shoes. Other attorneys work here, but she has no partners. That would give somebody else a measure of control and a financial stake in the firm. Raisa Volkov does not share authority.

The most annoying part of all is that I still admire her. She built this firm from the ground up and made a name for herself, not only in New York, but around the country.

Yeah, I'm a pathetic fangirl.

"Elena!"

Oh great. Her Royal Highness is summoning me. I rotate my chair toward her office door and smile politely. "Good morning, Raisa. What can I do for you?"

"Why don't I have the Caldwell case file? Someone didn't put it on my desk this morning."

"Someone" hadn't gotten out the file because another someone hadn't said she needed it.

Raisa jabs a finger in the air in my general direction. "Go get it."

Naturally, the most obnoxious woman in New York looks like a supermodel. She has long legs and a slender body, with ebony hair that glistens beautifully and skin that glows even in lighting conditions that make me look sallow. According to the male interns, her dark eyes lend her an aura of mystery.

She storms up to me dressed in her Armani pantsuit, towering over me in a way that makes me feel like a munchkin, and taps one finger on my desk. "Why aren't you getting that file? Go. Now."

"Yes, Raisa. Right away."

I scurry off to the file room and retrieve the documents she wants. Everything is on the firm's servers, but lawyers seem to have a weird aversion to looking at files on their computers. They even take notes on pads of paper, instead of digital tablets. That leaves us paralegals and interns to brave the dusty, windowless file room to get whatever the attorneys need.

At least the maze of cubicles where we all work gets some sunlight, even if it's secondhand. The attorneys' offices rim the cubicle zone, and every office has large windows. The glass walls can be turned opaque by flipping a switch, but most of the time they're clear, giving the grunt workers a touch of natural light.

When I get back to my desk, I see Raisa's office door is shut. I swig my cold coffee, then approach her door. Just as I raise my hand to knock, the door swings inward.

"There you are," Raisa says, like she's been waiting hours for me to come back. It's been ten minutes. She snatches the file out of my hand. "Get in here. We need to talk."

A sour taste creeps into my mouth. She's about to fire me. On day three.

Cursed, for sure.

I dutifully walk into her office. When she shuts the door, I flinch. I feel like a peasant about to be guillotined, and the thump of the door was that giant blade lopping off someone else's head. Next up, me.

Raisa points at one of two chairs positioned in front of her desk. "Sit."

A man stands at the window, facing away from us. The sunshine burnishes his blond hair with streaks of molten gold.

I flump onto the chair.

Raisa settles onto her large executive chair behind the desk. "I've hired someone to replace Lucas Miller."

Though I've never met Lucas Miller, I've heard the office gossip about him. He handled corporate law before he quit suddenly a few days before I started my job here.

Raisa waves a hand negligently toward the man who still faces away from us. "Meet Lucas's replacement, Chance Dixon."

The man pivots on his heels to face me.

A tingle sweeps over my entire body, and I suddenly can't take in a whole breath. I stammer something resembling "hello," though what comes out of my mouth isn't actually a word.

The sexy Brit from the hotel stares at me, his face blank.

I stare right back at him, probably looking like a stupefied moron.

Raisa doesn't seem to notice our reactions to each other.

Damn, he looks even better than Friday night, dressed in a navy suit that brings out the color of his eyes and accentuates the panty-melting beauty of his body. It ought to be illegal to look so good.

His blank stare dissolves into a smile that curves his lips little by little, heating up with every millimeter his mouth moves. His gaze warms too, burning into me with the heat of the midday sun toasting my bare skin. One side of his mouth kinks upward more than the other in the sexiest lopsided smile I've ever seen.

My lips curl up at the corners, while my body rouses the way it had Friday night, readying for whatever this man wants to do to me.

We're in the office. With my boss. And I am getting more and more turned on just looking at Chance Dixon.

Still oblivious, Raisa motions for Chance to sit in the chair beside me.

I try not to stare anymore, but honestly, I only have so much willpower. When he passes by me, his ass is an arm's length from my face. I've never seen him naked, but I've had my leg strapped around him and felt those taut, powerful glutes.

He settles that perfect bottom onto the chair beside me, propping one ankle on the other knee.

Raisa smiles at him with all the flirtatiousness of a teenager, even batting her eyelashes. "I'm so pleased you've finally come home to our firm, where you belong." She aims her businesswoman smile at me. "Chance is my husband."

"Ex-husband," he corrects.

The lovely blush of desire that warmed my entire body snuffs out. Her ex-husband? She'd called him husband, no ex. Coupled with the way she batted her lashes at him, that implies she doesn't think of him as her former spouse, but as hers, period.

Fantastic. I had a quickie in an elevator with the ex-husband of my bitchy boss who hates me, and she wants him back. Does he want her back too? If he volunteered to work here, he must want to be close to her. Why did he seduce me the other night? A divorce lawyer who's a cheater. Doesn't that just figure.

Nope, my luck has not changed one bit.

Back in the hotel, I'd hoped his name, Chance, might be a good omen or something. Wrong. The dice got tossed, and I hit snake eyes.

Raisa waves her hand in the way I've already figured out means she's dismissing me. "Elena, you will work exclusively with Chance until I say otherwise. Do whatever he says. Chance, think of her as your slave."

I glance sideways at him.

He smirks at me while he tells my boss, "Thank you, Raisa. I've always wanted a slave of my own."

The boss lady is focused on the papers on her desk, ignoring us. Once she dismisses you, all that's left to do is walk out the door. I'd learned this about Raisa Volkov after two full days as her slave.

Now she's handing me over to Chance. As *his* slave. My body loves the idea, but my brain keeps warning me to watch out.

Chance opens the door for me as we exit Raisa's office. He lays a hand on the small of my back, guiding me toward the office that previously belonged to Lucas Miller. They must have changed the sign on the door early this morning, because it now says "Chance Dixon."

He holds the door open for me. "Slaves enter first."

I want to scowl at him, but I pull myself together and stay professional. "Thank you, Mr. Dixon."

"Call me Chance."

"Rather not. Sir." It's dumb, but I hope calling him mister and sir will put some kind of distance between us.

Yeah, I said it was dumb.

He shuts the door while I take a seat in front of his desk, then he sits down in the spiffy executive chair. The office is spacious, though not as big as Raisa's. This is her firm, after all. Still, Chance's office features large windows that catch the morning sun at the perfect angle to make his gorgeous face look even more beautiful. The rays of golden sunshine kiss his skin, spilling down his face, onto his throat.

"I had no idea you worked here," he says. "But I'm glad to see you. After the way you ran off—"

"No running. I walked. And you never called me, so you're the one who has explaining to do."

"You gave me the wrong number. I had a lovely conversation with the owner of an Italian deli, but he didn't know any Elena." Chance rocks his chair slowly, keeping his focus on me. "I wondered if you gave me the wrong number on purpose."

"I wouldn't do that. Sorry I got it wrong, but I was kind of, um, confused." I fidget in my chair, which seems to be made of pins and needles. Or maybe that sensation is a figment of my freaking-out mind. "After hearing you argue with somebody on the phone, I started to think I'd made a big mistake."

"Do you still feel that way? Because I don't. I wanted more time with you."

His voice is soothing and stimulating at the same time, an odd combination that compels me to relax. "I don't regret it."

"I'm glad." He sinks back in his chair, shoulders slumped, and rubs his eyes. "It was Raisa on the phone that night."

And she's still into him. That much is obvious.

Does he want to reconcile with her?

Chance drops his hand, fixing me with an earnest look. "I shouldn't have shagged you in an elevator. But you were the most enchanting, sexiest woman I'd ever seen, and I had to have you. I've never done anything of the sort before."

I shrug. "What's done is done. I'm your employee now, which means it's strictly business between us from this moment on. Agreed?"

He studies me, those sapphire eyes sparking in the sunlight. "I don't want only business with you, Elena."

I love the way he says my name in that delicious British accent, with that husky timbre in his voice. Though my body wants me to crawl across the desk and curl up on his lap, I straighten, clear my throat, and say, "Strictly business. Please. I need this job, and my boss is clearly still in love with you."

"But I'm not in love with her." He strokes the smooth desktop with his long fingers, caressing it like he's making love to the polished wood. "I want you, Elena, not her. If it weren't completely inappropriate, I'd have you on this desk right now."

My body reaffirms its desire to do anything he wants, making me feel warm all over. No way will I have sex with him at work. Never going to happen. Never, never, never.

I gaze into his eyes, and his lips slide into a soft smile.

Not today, at least.

"Please have dinner with me," he says. "Let me make up for my behavior the other night."

Holy heaven, I want to say yes. Dinner with a sexy, gorgeous, charming British man? Double yes, count me in. But I have to say no.

"That would be inappropriate," I say. "You're my boss."

"I agree, but I can't resist a woman who knows at least twelve German numbers and who makes me so hard I could pound nails into a wall with my cock."

A laugh splutters out of me. "That's the silliest thing I've ever heard."

He grins. "At least I made you laugh."

It's not fair for him to be so cute and so swoon-worthy at the same time.

"Our relationship has to be professional," I tell him. "Nothing more."

He sighs. "All right, I'll give it a go. But I can't stop myself from wanting you, and I can't swear I won't at least try to kiss you."

"I'm sure you can restrain yourself if you really work at it."

"For you, I'll try anything." He leans back in his chair, but his fingers still stroke the desktop. "Raisa has it wrong. I am *your* slave, Miss Linwood."

Having no clue what to say to that, I excuse myself and head back to my desk in the cubicle zone.

And I keep thinking about him.

Chapter Three

Chance

I show extraordinary willpower by keeping my hands off Elena for a full three hours. But honestly, it's her fault when my resolve slips. I call her to ask for a file, and she says she'll bring it to me. A few seconds later, she sashays past the open door of my office on her way to the file room, hips swaying, head held high. A slight smile tugs at her mouth, but she doesn't glance my way. The sight of her tight arse and those breasts, covered but not really concealed by her clothes, does me in. I grab a paperweight off my desk and fist my hand around it. Loosen my fist. Tighten it. Loosen. Tighten.

But in my mind, I'm closing my hand around one of those perfect breasts.

Maybe I haven't seen her naked yet and don't actually know what her breasts look like, but I'm positive they are perfect. Elena Linwood has curves in all my favorite places and a mouth that I loved kissing.

How can I work with her and never touch her again?

I should resign immediately, then drag Elena into the nearest closet and shag her until she screams.

But I can't. First of all, it would be very wrong. After the way I behaved on Friday night, I want to prove to Elena I'm not an arse who cares only about his own pleasure. Second, I promised Raisa I'd help her with her little problem. If she thinks she can use this situation to seduce me into taking her back, she will be severely disappointed. I don't love her anymore. I respect her legal skills and determination, and I know deep down she's not a rotten bitch. Still, I don't approve of the way she's been treating her employees lately. Maybe I can convince her to stop taking her frustrations out on them. I'm the reason she's acting this way, so it's my responsibility to set things right.

How the bloody hell will I pull that off?

Maybe I should've accepted Garth Leonard's offer. I'd be in New Hampshire now, far away from Raisa.

And Elena.

No, I don't want to be anywhere else.

Elena sashays into my office and sets the file on my desk. "Here's the information you need, sir. Do you require anything else?"

Yes, I require her spread across my desk naked.

Shaking off the sinful idea, even though I love it, I wave toward the chairs on her side of the desk. "Sit, Elena, please. I'd like to talk to you."

She eyes the chairs, the most endearing crinkle forming between her brows, but then sits down—on the edge of the chair, like she plans on fleeing any second.

"This is awkward, I know," I tell her. "But pretending we haven't met before, haven't known each other intimately before, isn't the answer."

"What we did wasn't intimate. It was a quickie with a stranger."

"I like you, Elena. Is that a crime?"

She gets that sweet little crinkle again, making me want to kiss it away. "No offense, Mr. Dixon, but you don't know me. I don't know you either."

"Oh, I know a few relevant facts about you." I retrieve a folder from a drawer and lay it open on the desk. "I know you're twenty-seven, single, and you share an apartment with your brother. You grew up in a small town in Wisconsin and graduated from Northwestern, summa cum laude. You were accepted to Columbia Law School but backed out. Since you had already moved to New York by that point, you stayed and worked as a secretary in a law office until you received your paralegal certification."

She stares at me for several seconds, not blinking, her hands clamped over her knees. "How do you know all that?"

"Raisa is very thorough. Before she hires anyone, she has a complete background check done on them." I tap the open folder. "This is yours. Raisa gave it to me."

"That's… kind of creepy."

"It's business. Raisa is, admittedly, rather paranoid." I close the file. "But I want to know more about you, all the things that don't show up in a background check."

"Do I get to run a background check on you?"

"No need." I lean back in my chair. "Ask me anything you like."

"How about all the same facts you have on me?"

"Of course." I keep my gaze on hers while I speak, entranced by the deep caramel color of her eyes. "I'm thirty-four, divorced, not seeing anyone at the moment." I smile and wink. "Unless you agree to have dinner with me."

She shakes her head, though a smile she's trying to prevent dimples her cheeks. "Continue with the facts, please."

"All right. I grew up in the English countryside, in a quaint little village. I attended Oxford but got my law degree from Yale. I live alone. Since this job is only temporary, I'm staying in the hotel across the street, the one where you and I met." I shrug one shoulder. "I didn't graduate with honors, like you, but I did well enough academically. I've been working for a medium-size firm in Chicago, but I've taken a sabbatical to lend a hand here."

"Until Raisa hires a permanent replacement for Lucas Miller." When I nod, she asks, "What exactly happened with him?"

I'm about to say I can't talk about that when I realize there's no good reason to be cagey. The animosity between Raisa and Lucas isn't a secret, though Elena might not have heard about it yet. She only started working here on Thursday, which I know because Raisa told me.

"Ten days ago, Lucas Miller resigned," I say. Miller had turned up at Raisa's apartment Saturday a week ago to deliver his resignation in person, resulting in an argument so loud that her neighbors called the police, but I shouldn't tell Elena that part. "Lucas never got on with Raisa, and her recent behavior pushed him over the edge. He quit without notice. That left Raisa in a desperate situation, since several of Lucas's clients have court dates coming up soon."

"That's why you're here."

"Yes. I'm the emergency reinforcements. I've done a fair bit of corporate law, so I was qualified to take over as lead counsel."

"I thought attorneys couldn't quit a case unless the client's doing something wrong."

"That's true," I say, and decide I ought to tell her the whole story after all. She'll be my right hand on these cases, and she'll probably find out anyway via the office grapevine. "Lucas Miller didn't just resign. He was arrested ten days ago, on a Saturday night, after he went to Raisa's apartment and started screaming at her. He also tried to hit her, but she slammed the door in his face before he could. Lucas had a severe mental breakdown and was taken to the hospital."

"Holy cow. I had no idea. I heard somebody say he 'went off the deep end,' but I figured it was an exaggeration."

I shake my head. "Unfortunately, it's not. Raisa contacted a judge she knows well to get permission for me to take over Miller's cases."

"Now I feel kind of bad for thinking Raisa drives me crazy. I meant it as a metaphor, not the actual truth." Elena slides back in her chair and crosses her legs. "Raisa is a lot older than you, isn't she?"

"Yes, she's forty-eight. I imagine you read the *New Yorker* piece on her last year."

Elena nods. "The article described her as a powerhouse player on the New York legal scene. I already knew about her, though, about how she built her own firm from the ground up and became the queen of divorce court. That's why I wanted to become a lawyer, and it's why I wanted to work here. She's amazing." Elena twists her mouth into the most disarming expression of frustration. "The journalist who wrote that piece neglected to mention Raisa is a raging bitch."

"She wasn't like that until recently." I hesitate, wondering how much I should reveal to Elena, but if I want to see more of her, outside of work, I suppose I ought to share more with her. "Our divorce was finalized two months ago. Raisa has always been tough, sometimes rude, but she didn't become a raging bitch until the final decree came through. It's my fault she's been terrorizing the staff."

"Uh-huh," Elena says with a touch of suspicion. "Freshly divorced sounds like big-time trouble to me. Maybe you shouldn't screw other women until you and Raisa get over each other."

"I *am* over her. Have been for a long time. Our divorce might've been finalized two months ago, but we were separated for more than a year before that."

"Still don't want to get in the middle of your marital problems."

And I can't blame her for not wanting to get in the middle of it, but I've never met a woman who intrigues me the way Elena does. Or one who gets me randy the way she does. I want to know her better, but she won't let me. Working with Elena every day might kill me. At the very least, it will leave me with blue balls.

We watch each other for a moment, Elena seeming to size me up while I catalog all the things I love about her body. Full breasts, the kind that make me dream about all the things I can do to them with my mouth, my hands, and even my cock. Creamy skin with the faintest freckles on her face. Strong legs. I know that because she'd gripped me with one of those legs while I drove into her like a maniac. Her elegant fingers had clutched my head while I devoured her nipple. Her face is more than lovely, it's like a masterpiece of beauty sculpted by Michelangelo himself.

My curiosity gets the better of me, not for the first time, and I ask, "Why didn't you go to law school?"

"None of your damn business." She stands up and squares her shoulders. "What can I do for you this morning, Mr. Dixon? I'm sure you need to get up to speed with Lucas Miller's active cases."

I do, but that's the last thing I want to think about right now. Still, I rub my neck and say, "Yes, please pull all the files and bring them to me. I'll get started on the five hundred and thirty-two emails clogging my inbox."

"That's my job. I sort through them, delete the spam and other useless stuff, and let you know when it's safe to open your inbox."

"I appreciate that, Elena. Thank you."

"You're welcome." She turns toward the door, then hesitates. "Would you like coffee? I get Raisa's every morning."

"No, thank you. But I'd love a cuppa."

"A cup of what? You said no to coffee."

"Tea. That's what cuppa means."

Elena almost smiles. "I'm guessing that's the British way to say it. Sorry, but you are the first British person I've ever met. I don't think watching Henry Cavill movies counts."

"Probably not." I relax, really relax, for the first time since I arrived in New York. "I would love that cuppa, though. If it's not too much trouble."

"Of course not." Her cheeks dimple again. "I'm your slave, after all."

And fuck, just like that I'm imagining every possible scenario for making her my slave.

"Should I close the door or leave it open?" she asks.

"Leave it open."

Elena walks out the door, giving me a clear view of her luscious arse.

My desk phone rings.

The second I pick up the receiver, before I can speak one syllable, Raisa says, "I want you, Chance. Come to my office and take me on the desk."

My thoughts rewind to a few minutes ago, when I'd fantasized about doing exactly that with Elena.

"No, Raisa," I say. "We've been through this before, ad nauseam. I don't want you anymore."

"Oh come on," she purrs, "we both know that's not true."

"It is."

And I'm not lying. Part of me will always care about Raisa, as a friend, but I stopped feeling any attraction to her a long time ago. Maybe I'd been so desperate to shag Elena on Friday night because I hadn't been with anyone since the last time Raisa and I had sex.

"I'm doing you a favor here," I tell Raisa. "Don't make me regret it."

"Please tell me you're not doing a barista or, heaven forbid, a call girl."

"None of the above." True, since Elena is neither of those things. Besides, I'm not technically doing her, not anymore. Maybe soon, I hope, but not yet. "This is strictly business, Raisa. Now, let me get to work on solving your unfortunate problem. Enjoy your black coffee."

I hang up on my ex-wife.

Earlier today, Elena had told me our relationship is strictly business, but the difference is that I meant it when I said those words to Raisa. Elena doesn't mean it. She can't. Not after what we did the other night. I scratch under my collar but can't eradicate the itch. How can I ever start something with Elena with Raisa down the hall, a few doors away? I need to get Elena alone, outside of the office, but she isn't having any of it.

As if on cue, Elena sashays into my office again, this time carrying a plastic tray. It holds a mug, packets of sugar, a small carton of milk, and a plastic spoon. While she comes closer, I notice the tray also holds a cookie lying on a white napkin.

Elena sets the tray on my desk, careful to keep that bloody piece of furniture between us. "Your tea, Mr. Dixon. I know this probably isn't how you Brits do teatime, but it's the best we've got here in the good old US of A."

"It's wonderful, thank you." I pick up the mug, reading the words painted on it. "The law is hot. Am I meant to read between the lines?"

"No, it's a novelty mug, nothing more. You're lucky I didn't give you the one that says 'you can bang my gavel anytime.' I think an intern left that one here."

I set down the mug and pick up the cookie.

"Brits like tea and biscuits, right?" she asks. "And biscuits are cookies, aren't they? If not, then I've been seriously misled by all those BBC shows I watched."

"This is perfect." I take a bite of the cookie. Uh, biscuit. Maybe I've been in America too long. The distinctive flavor fills my mouth, and I lift one brow. "Peanut butter?"

"Sorry, that's all I could find." She tilts forward a touch, peering down at my mug. "I hope the tea is okay, because all we have is Earl Grey or eggnog flavor. I'm sure that one's been lying around since Christmas. So I figured you'd prefer Earl Grey."

I pour milk into my tea and take a sip. "Just right. Thank you."

She wrinkles her nose, making her upper lip pucker. "No sugar?"

"No."

"Yech," she says, her nose twitching like the thought of un-sweetened tea is about to make her sneeze.

I chuckle. "You really are the most adorable creature."

"Better get those files," she says, and marches out the door.

To hell with Raisa. I want Elena. Now.

But the phone rings, and I need to take the call. It's a client, after all.

Somehow, I will convince Elena to have dinner with me. I have to, or else I'll be the next attorney at Raisa Volkov & Associates who leaps off the deep end.

Chapter Four

Elena

When I take an armload of files to Chance's office, he's on the phone, so I drop them off and leave. Thank goodness he's busy. If I hear his voice anymore, I will go insane. The way he says my name gives me hot shivers. His accent makes my knees weak. When he smirks at me, I go instantly wet and hot between my thighs. But if he looks at me again, with that smoldering intensity, I will lose it. I might just hump him right there on his desk.

Shit. What is wrong with me?

I'm an adult. A strong, independent woman with career goals. I finally landed my dream job, and I won't screw that up by screwing the boss's ex-husband. Resistance would be easier if he weren't so nice, so charming, so… British.

He'd called me adorable. Twice.

And both times, hearing those words tumble from his nibble-worthy lips made me long to do anything he wanted. I had done that Friday night, but things are different today.

No nibbling on my boss's ex. Check.

Ten minutes before one—the time when Raisa and I both take our lunch breaks, separately—she calls me into her office. I take a seat on the peasant side of the desk, while Raisa sits regally upright on the queen side.

"You are very capable," she says. "I've been impressed with your work so far."

She paid me a compliment. Wow. "Thank you, Raisa."

"I feel I can trust you with a special assignment. It requires total confidentiality. I'm relying on you, Elena, so don't disappoint me."

No pressure there. None at all.

My stomach is twisting into knots, but so what?

"I appreciate that," I say. "I won't let you down."

Could she be about to let me in on the Hazelton case? It's the biggest divorce in New York in a decade, maybe longer.

"Here's what I need you to do," Raisa says. "Convince Chance to come back to me."

For a couple seconds that feels like an hour, I gape at her—on the inside. A good paralegal never shows her true horror. "I don't quite understand what you're asking."

I understand, but I can't believe it. Maybe I hallucinated it.

"Chance and I belong together," she says. "Letting him go was a terrible mistake, and I know I can get him back. With your help."

"Um, what exactly do you want me to do?"

"First, find out if he's dating or sleeping with anyone. If so, I need all the details you can wheedle out of him." She eyes me like I'm a cow being auctioned off for meat. "You're passably pretty. Use your feminine wiles to get him to open up to you. Honestly, I don't care what you do as long as you find out what I need to know. Then we can move on to step two."

As much as I really, really don't want to know, I ask, "What's step two?"

"You talk me up to Chance and convince him he belongs with me."

Fabulous. This is exactly the career move I need, becoming pimp and marriage counselor for my boss.

Who also happens to be the ex-wife of the guy I let bang my gavel Friday night.

Yep, I'm cursed.

"What do you think?" Raisa asks, looking at me expectantly, almost excited.

Jeez, what can I say? She's my boss, and getting fired after three days will not improve my resume. "Sure, I'll do it. Anything to help."

"Thank you, Elena." She leans forward, her tone and expression turning conspiratorial. "This is strictly between us. Confidential."

"Of course." I make a zipper motion across my mouth. "My lips are sealed."

While I push myself up out of the chair, Raisa rushes around her desk to where I stand.

And she throws her arms around me.

"I knew you were the kind of woman who would understand," she says while clinching me tighter. "I'm so grateful, Elena. You're an angel."

Yeah, I feel like total crap inside. Like I'm the scum that grows in a toilet that's been ripped out and tossed into a garbage dump in a swamp. That's me, Elena the green, slimy scum. What kind of "angel" agrees to help her boss win back her ex-husband, when that "angel" has done the deed with her ex-husband?

Cursed. Damned. Nauseous. I'm all those things.

I'm so getting fired.

Raisa lets go of me, and I swear her eyes are shimmering with almost-tears. She retreats behind her desk, swiveling her chair to face the window, to face away from me.

After about thirty seconds of silence, I decide she's dismissed me, and I leave.

Since I brown-bagged lunch today, I walk a few blocks to a little park where I can sit and eat in solitude. When I get back to the office, Raisa is eating Chinese takeout in her office. I almost go in there to ask if she needs anything, but Raisa reassigned me to be Chance's slave. I don't work for her, not for the time being. I belong to the sexy Brit.

Every time I think about that, my entire body tingles.

No sex with Chance. Get that out of your head, woman.

Right. No sex. No fondling. No kissing.

Ogling is allowed, though. Right? I mean, what harm can come from me drooling over him, as long as nobody sees me doing it? If a tree falls in the forest and no one hears it, the tree never fell, right? And yes, in this ridiculous metaphor, Chance Dixon is a tree. Well, his dick certainly gets stiff enough to pass for a tree. And it's thick like a big, hard oak, and—

Stop that this instant.

I tiptoe up to Chance's office door, hoping to see he's not back from lunch yet. At least then I'll have a brief reprieve from needing to fight my lustful urges. Jeez, it's barely been half a day. How am I going to survive weeks? Maybe months?

Just my luck, he's in his office—and he catches me peeking around the doorjamb at him.

Chance smiles, in that so-damn-sexy way. "There's my slave. Would you care to wash my feet?"

Yes, with my tongue. Not only his feet, but every inch of his body.

"Oh please," I say, rolling my eyes as I step into the office. "I just got back from lunch and wanted to see if you need anything."

"Actually, yes, I do." His gaze roves up and down my body, and his tongue slips out to wet his lips. He clears his throat, swerving his attention down to the papers on his desk. Gathering them up, he offers them to me. "Would you mind going through these depositions and drafting a summary?"

"Sure thing." Hallelujah, work to do that doesn't involve pimping or lying. I snatch the papers from him and make a beeline for the door.

"Elena."

My tummy flutters, and my knees wobble the teeniest bit. Oh God, I wish he'd never say my name again.

And I wish he'd say it every five seconds.

Yeah, I'm flip-flopping like a beached whale.

I paste on my professional smile and face him. "Yes, Mr. Dixon?"

He sighs, tapping his pen on the desktop. "Do I have to order you to call me Chance? I don't like being called mister."

"Sorry. I was trying to be professional and respectful."

"And I appreciate that, but it's not necessary."

I realize I've hurt his feelings, and I feel bad about that. My stupid idea to create distance between us by calling him Mr. Dixon is done. I rewind the conversation and start again. "What do you need, Chance?"

"For you to have dinner with me."

Damn, I want to say yes so badly. "I can't. The firm has a policy about coworkers dating."

"Yes, and it says all that's required is reporting the relationship to Raisa within thirty days. We have plenty of time to worry about that later, if things work out between us."

If things work out. I don't see how that can happen. He's my boss's ex, and she commanded me to help her get him back.

"No, I'm sorry, Chance. I can't get involved with you."

Spinning around, I hurry out of his office. How can I even think about having dinner with him? It was bad enough when he was my boss's ex-husband. Now, not only is he my boss's ex, but I've been tasked with convincing him to go back to her. I've got to stay away from Chance as much as possible.

Luckily, summarizing the depositions takes the rest of the afternoon.

Unfortunately, that means when I come to work the next morning, I have to venture into Chance's office again to ask what he needs me to do today. Since erotic dreams about him plagued my sleep, I'm in less than top form this morning, so frazzled in fact that I forgot to stop at Starbucks and buy a latte. How can I survive the morning without my coffee? The stuff in the break room is terrible.

Before I even attempt to see Chance, I need caffeine. With a choice between terrible coffee and a cup of tea, I go for the tea. I even brew Chance a cup, then drop my mug off at my desk while I take the other mug into his office.

He's sitting behind his desk, forehead crinkled, staring at a document.

I place his mug on the desk beside the document. "Good morning, Chance. I thought you might need it, so I brought you a cuppa."

And I'm so damn proud of myself for remembering the British word for a cup of tea.

He glances up at me and smiles a little, his forehead smoothing out. Taking a sip of tea, he studies me. "Thank you, Elena. You look incredible this morning. In my dreams last night, we had a very good time."

"You shouldn't say things like that at work. Someone might overhear."

"Yes, and then Raisa might fire me." He says that with a twinkle in his gorgeous blue eyes and an amused slant to his lips. "I'm sure you can console me when that happens. I've already fantasized about you doing that."

I really, really, really need to tell him to stop flirting.

Before I crawl onto his lap and unzip his pants.

Yeah, I know what I *should* tell him, but my mouth has other ideas. Or maybe it's my hormones talking when I hear myself say, "You look pretty damn incredible too. And in my dreams, we had more than a good time. We rocked."

Chance grins, and every part of me that can melt does. "Why would you say something like that? You keep telling me we shouldn't have sex or even go out to dinner. But you're flirting with me." He sets down his mug and slants toward me. "And I love it."

"I didn't mean to. What I said was inappropriate, and I apologize." I'm totally lying, but who cares? This is too much fun. "How can I make it up to you?"

He pushes his chair back and pats his lap. "Come here, Elena."

My name. Again. Flowing from his kissable lips.

I want to go over there, but I don't dare try it. The door is open, and he hasn't darkened the windows, but I'm not at all convinced that will stop me from behaving in a very unprofessional manner. With him, I have zero willpower. Not one itty-bitty scrap of it.

"Work, Chance," I force myself to say. "This is a law office, not a strip club. What work do you need me to do for you?"

He sighs like I've said the most boring, annoying thing imaginable. "If you insist on doing your job, I have research for you to dig into."

I walk out of Chance's office five minutes later with enough research on my plate to keep me busy all week. I could almost cry from relief.

No more faltering willpower. Instead, I can hide out in law libraries.

Coward? Me? Nah.

Chapter Five

Chance

I've been acting like a sleazy lawyer. People make jokes about those kinds of lawyers, the ones who have no morals and no ethics, no compunctions about doing anything and everything to get what they want. I've prided myself on being a decent bloke who happens to be an attorney, and my clients appreciate that. Raisa has always thought I was too rigid and ought to bend my ethics now and then. Not break them, but simply stretch the boundaries a little in the name of serving my clients' interests. I refuse to do that.

Yet here I am sexually harassing a paralegal.

Granted, I'd met Elena before I started working here. We had sex a few days ago, and I still can't wrap my head around the idea she works for my ex-wife and now for me, temporarily. How can I not flirt with Elena? I've kissed her, fondled her, fucked her. I know more about her body than any employer has a right to know, but I can't erase Friday night from history. I don't want to, anyway.

Sure, the firm's policy on dating gives me leeway. But I'm technically her boss, which pushes me into a gray area.

I have to stop my inappropriate behavior—at work.

How can I convince her to see me outside of the office? I can't figure out how to arrange that when I've resolved to behave like a professional, ethical attorney.

"Fuck," I hiss under my breath.

Elena disappears for the rest of the day, no doubt ensconced in a law library somewhere.

I try my damnedest not to think about her, but it's like trying not to breathe. Elena Linwood is temptation incarnate, not to mention being sweet and competent and thoughtful. She'd brought me tea this morning, voluntarily. I survive the entire day, managing to do my job despite fantasizing about the sexiest paralegal I've ever met.

At ten o'clock, I decide I've worked long enough today. Raisa is still in her office when I shut the door to mine. I can tell by the light leaking out around her office door, though she's turned the windows opaque so I can't see into the room. My hopes of skulking out of here without needing to speak to her are shattered when I'm halfway to the elevator and her office door opens, spilling light across the array of cubicles and all the way to the elevator.

"Chance," Raisa calls out. "I need to speak to you. Immediately."

I growl, too softly for Raisa to hear. Why hadn't I left five minutes earlier? She might not have noticed then.

"I'm knackered, Raisa," I say as I turn sideways to glance at her. "Whatever it is can wait until morning."

She disappears into her office for a few seconds, long enough that I almost believe she's given up. Then she emerges again, her purse slung over her shoulder, and shuts off the light. Only the ambient glow from outside the windows illuminates the space as she trots down the center aisle of the cubicle farm and straight to me.

"Let's have dinner in your hotel room," she says. "We can talk there."

"No. This is my relaxation time." And my time away from her. "I'm off the clock until morning."

She makes a noise that implies I'm an idiot. "Lawyers are never really off the clock."

"This one is."

"Don't be this way, Chance." She runs her hands up and down my lapels, inching closer and closer until her body almost touches mine. "After a long day of working, we both need to blow off some steam. And you have a nice big suite right across the street."

When I'd first met Raisa, she had been the sexiest woman on earth to me. These days, I can't look at her without remembering the things she did to drive me away. I don't want to speak to her, much less take her to my hotel room.

All I want is Elena.

"Forget it," I tell Raisa. "That ship sailed and sank a long time ago. The me who wanted you drowned in the wreck."

I might have stretched that metaphor a bit too far.

Raisa moves to kiss me.

"Leave off," I say, pushing her away. "Try to remember I'm doing you a favor by working here."

Her expression hardens, the way it always does when I deny her something she wants. "Who are you sleeping with, Chance? You must be doing someone."

"Even if I am, it's none of your concern." The fact that I frequently want to throw Elena over my desk and ravish her has no bearing on this conversation. "Good night, Raisa. I'll see you in the morning."

Thankfully, the elevator doors slide open.

I step into the car.

And thankfully, Raisa doesn't follow me.

Like a pathetic, divorced man, I spend the evening eating pizza and drinking beer, then drop onto the bed and fall asleep on top of the covers. I don't get drunk. That's not what a trustworthy lawyer does at night, not even when his ex-wife has tried to seduce him and the woman he wants in his bed has said no. Two beers is my maximum. I sleep on top of the covers strictly because I'm too exhausted to give a damn.

Naturally, I dream of Elena.

I wake up harder than usual in the morning and need a thirty-minute shower to get rid of my lust for the delectable paralegal. I rub one off three times before I feel ready to face the world.

And the woman whose voluptuous body caused the problem.

When I arrive at work, Raisa is the only one there. She's in her office with the door closed, and I do not bother saying good morning. After her actions last night, I have no desire to see or speak to her. I've just gotten my cuppa from the break room when Elena turns up. Some of the other employees got here a few minutes before her, though she's still early. The workday officially starts at nine, but she's here at eight.

Elena smiles brightly at her coworkers, laughing and talking with them while she makes her way to her cubicle while carrying a Starbucks cup in her hand. She's beautiful. Alive. Sexy. Elena Linwood burns like a brilliant flame, and I want to bask in the heat and light she gives off.

Apparently, I've turned into a bad poet as well as a smitten fool.

Locking myself in my office seems like the best course to avoid a sexual harassment charge. If I speak to Elena, I might not be able to stop myself from telling her how desirable she is.

Fuckable is a better description of her. Completely fuckable.

At lunchtime, I peek out of my office like the coward I've become.

Elena is still at her desk, poring over some sort of work. She lifts her head at the exact moment I look at her and smiles, waving her fingers at me.

I nod and retreat into my office.

She appears at my doorway a few seconds later. "I was going to order some lunch, Chinese delivery. Do you want some?"

Lunch with Elena. That sounds wonderful, but likely to get me disbarred.

"We're all having a working lunch," she says. "You can join the plebs in the conference room, if you want."

"Plebs? This isn't ancient Rome, and I'm not the emperor."

"No, that would be Raisa." Elena's cheeks dimple, which always makes me want to kiss her. "But I am your slave, remember?"

She speaks those words in a soft, sensual tone, clearly flirting with me.

I want to spend time in her presence, even if it's a group lunch. "All right. Count me in."

"Good." She smiles, the expression lighting up her face. "You'll like the gang. They're not uptight or anything."

Elena leaves me, and I wait a few minutes before heading to the conference room. I need those minutes to convince myself this isn't a rubbish idea. I should meet more of the staff and get to know them a bit, show them I'm not the empress's consort who does her bidding. I've always tried to be an approachable boss. Here's my chance to prove that to my new coworkers.

Yes, that's right. I'm being a good boss. This has nothing whatsoever to do with Elena and her perfect tits.

When I walk into the conference room, all heads swivel toward me. And the conversation stops dead.

Elena gets up and lays a hand on my arm. "You all know Chance Dixon. He's taking over Lucas Miller's cases. I invited Chance to our little working lunch, so let's make him feel welcome."

I feel oddly uncomfortable, what with a dozen people staring at me, so I pat my stomach and say, "Where's the food? I'm ready to pass out from hunger."

"It'll be here any minute," Elena says.

My attempt to seem like an average person, not an evil lawyer, seems to have crashed and burned. Everyone is still staring at me.

I try a different tack. "Who wants to play pin the tail on the lawyer's arse?"

"Me," says a young man at the other end of the table, raising his hand.

Several more hands shoot up, and I'm beginning to wonder what I've let myself in for.

"Instead of shoving pins in Chance," Elena says, "why don't we tell him what we've all been working on? Jared, you can start. You've got the McNulty case, right?"

"Yeah," says the young man who'd been first to volunteer to shove a pin in my arse.

Elena urges me to sit beside her, and somehow, I manage to keep myself from sneaking a hand onto her thigh. The food arrives a few minutes later. For the next forty-five minutes, I eat the best Chinese food I've ever had while discussing the firm's cases with the paralegals who do most of the real work. Elena is the brightest by far, but the others have impressive legal acumen too. Elena jumps in to help her coworkers hash out research problems, or to mediate disagreements between them.

I can't help watching her. Admiring her. Wishing I could fuck her right here on the conference room table in front of all these people. It's not simple lust, though, not anymore. I'm coming to appreciate the clever mind behind the beautiful face and body.

After lunch, we all go back to our assigned desks.

Work keeps me occupied for the rest of the day, and I don't see Elena until it's nearly lunchtime the next day. She's been at the law library again, doing all the research I commanded her to do for me. Now, I wish I'd commanded her to take dictation in my office instead. Not seeing her, not hearing her voice out there in the cubicle farm, it makes me feel…anxious. Which is ridiculous. But here I am, chewing on the end of my very expensive gold pen while I wonder what Elena is doing right now.

Finally, I give up and go to her. She has a Starbucks cup on her desk, with her name scrawled on it.

"What are you drinking?" I ask.

She glances up at me, smiling in a distracted way. "Morning. I always have a butterscotch latte."

"That's not coffee."

"Maybe not for people who don't put sugar in their tea, but for the rest of humanity, it is."

Leaning against the cubicle wall, I study her. "It's not morning, Elena. It's lunchtime. You need to take a break."

"Oh, I brought a bag lunch today." She picks up a depressingly brown paper sack that's slumped on her desk and shakes it. "See? I'm all set. Have a good lunch, Chance."

I grab the extra chair that's shoved into the far corner of her tiny cubicle and set it down an arm's length from where she sits. My arse barely fits on the flimsy plastic-and-metal contraption. "It's lunch, Elena, not an invitation to an orgy. I want to confer with my paralegal over a meal."

Her lips tighten in a sexy little smile even while she types on her keyboard. "Sure, you want to confer with me."

Her tone implies something very, very wrong and very, very filthy.

Can she read my mind?

"Just lunch," I say. "Think of it as a business meeting."

"Right, business." She throws me a sly sideways glance. "You're all business whenever we're alone, aren't you?"

"We won't be alone. I'll take you to my favorite bistro, where there will be plenty of other people and plenty of light. No dark corners, I swear. We can sit by the window, if you like."

I want dark corners and a smoky atmosphere, with sensual music playing in the background. I want to do filthy things to her anytime, anywhere. But I promised myself I would not make any advances.

Today. Tomorrow is another story.

She still seems reluctant, though I sense she might be wavering.

"Relax," I say. "I'm British, remember? We say cheerio, and we love tea and crumpets. How much trouble could I possibly get you into?"

"Playing on American stereotypes of Brits? That's cute, but not convincing." She folds her arms under her breasts, which makes me notice them even more. Leaning in, she whispers, "You are the man who seduced me in an elevator."

"Guilty as charged. Let me make it up to you."

She chews on her bottom lip while scrutinizing me.

I squirm in my horrid little chair while seconds tick by.

Elena sighs and dumps her brown bag into the trash bin under her desk. "All right. I'm yours for lunch."

My mind conjures up several different ways I could mold that statement into a come-on, but I resist the impulse. Instead, I remain calm and professional while we board the elevator.

As soon as the doors close, I say, "You really should take a chance more often."

She raises her delicate brows at me. "Is that a dopey pun about your name?"

"It was unintentional, I swear. I can't help that my name is also a commonly used word." I lean in so close I can see the darker rims around her caramel irises. "But for the record, this Chance loves to be taken."

Elena laughs and shakes her head.

Chapter Six

Elena

*C*hance takes me to a quaint little bistro ten blocks away from the office, one he swears nobody at the office knows about—except Raisa, and she only ever came here with him. She doesn't like the place, he says, so she'll never come back here. We sit by the picture windows, where we have a beautiful view of the skyline across the river, and he insists I sit beside him instead of across the table from him. When Chance examines the menu, he sighs and looks disappointed.

"What's wrong?" I ask. "Thought this was your favorite restaurant."

"It is, but I always lament their lack of British foods. I'd kill for some bangers and mash."

"Okay," I say like I have no idea what he's talking about, because I don't. "I'm guessing that's not some weird sex slang."

"No, it's weird food slang for sausage and mashed potatoes." He goes back to perusing the menu while he tells me, "I haven't had bangers and mash in ages."

"Why don't you cook that for yourself?"

He glances up at me, moving only his eyes. "My cooking skills begin and end with heating water for tea, and I do that in the microwave."

"Maybe I can figure out how to make bangers and mash for you." I say the words before I realize what I'm suggesting. I want to cook for him? Yeah, I kind of do. Huh. "Is it some special kind of thoroughly disgusting British sausage?"

"It can be any type of sausage." He fake-frowns at the menu. "What, no bubble and squeak? I may have to reconsider this as my favorite bistro."

"Bubble and squeak? You just made that up, didn't you?"

He smirks at me over the top of his menu. "No, I did not. My mother makes that the day after she cooks up a traditional roast dinner. She uses the leftovers to make bubble and squeak."

I give him a teasing smile. "Otherwise known as dumpster diving?"

"Very funny, but we don't dig through the rubbish bin for leftovers." He sneaks a hand under the table to grasp my knee. "Careful. If you keep harassing me, I might have to do something completely inappropriate."

We order our food, and I pretend to be disappointed when he orders a hamburger with French onion soup. It's not British, as I point out, but he puts his hand on my knee again to let me know he's about ready to get inappropriate with the snarky American sitting next to him. I order the same thing, earning a sarcastic comment from him about what a copycat I am.

Throughout lunch, we talk. About anything, everything, whatever pops into our heads. I learn that he comes from a middle-class family that owns a beautiful, historic home in the English countryside, but when he asks about my family, I avoid answering. It would spoil the mood, and I love this mood we've got going here in the cutest bistro I've never seen before. He lets me get away with not opening up, at least for a while. We make each other laugh, a lot, and commiserate about working with Raisa.

Five minutes before we have to go back to the office, Chance finally pushes me for an answer to a question he asked me the first day we worked together. "Why didn't you go to law school?"

"What?" I'm acting dumb to avoid answering, obviously.

"You heard the question." He turns his chair slightly toward me. "You're very clever, hard-working, and write the most perfect legal summaries I've ever read. If I asked you to write an argument, I'm sure that would be perfect too. You should be an attorney, not a paralegal. I know you were accepted to law school, so why didn't you go?"

I slump in my chair, absently stirring the teeny puddle in my soup bowl, all that's left of my lunch. I can't look at him when I explain, "My dad ran out on us when I was six. I barely remember him. Mom worked two jobs to support me and my brother, Kyle. Six years ago, she got sick. Cancer. For eleven months, she fought so hard to beat it, but she couldn't. She died a week before I found out I'd been accepted to law school."

Chance settles his hand on my knee again, but he's not copping a feel this time. "I'm so sorry, Elena."

I shrug one shoulder. "I'd already gone into debt to pay for my bachelor's degree. Mom had life insurance, but not a lot of it. Racking up even more debt to pay for law school seemed like a huge extravagance, and besides, I had to take care of Kyle. He was fifteen at the time. So, I gave up on law school, got a crappy job as a legal secretary, and signed up for a paralegal certification course. Took me eighteen months to finish it. Working for Raisa is the second paralegal position I've had." I laugh a little, with no humor whatsoever. "It was my dream job."

"You excel at your job. Don't let Raisa ruin it for you. She'll calm down once she gets over the divorce and accepts that I am never going to be with her again."

I wince, unable to disguise my discomfort. How can I not tell him what Raisa ordered me to do? He deserves to know, but I can't tell him. Raisa ordered me to keep it secret. I don't know how long she'll wait for me to bring him to her on a silver platter.

How on earth does she expect me to do that, anyway? Even if I wanted to, which I absolutely do not, I have no clue where to start.

"What's wrong?" Chance asks.

"Can't tell you. Raisa swore me to secrecy."

He drums his fingers on the tabletop. "Does this secret have something to do with me? Is that the real reason you've been reluctant to get involved with me?"

"I can't say."

Chance scoots his chair a little closer to mine. "Look at me."

"Please let this go. I could lose my job."

"If this involves me, then I have a right to know. Raisa won't fire you, because I won't tell her I know the secret. All right?"

Chewing my lip, I think about what I should do. Not telling him has been eating a hole in my stomach, but telling him might make things worse. I like Chance, a lot. He's such a nice man, and he's been so sweet to me. But he's my boss's ex-husband, and she wants him back.

I groan miserably. "Raisa ordered me to help her win you back."

"She what?" he says sharply, his gaze narrowing. "What exactly did she tell you to do?"

"Whatever it takes to find out if you're sleeping with someone, and if so, who it is. I'm also supposed to say stuff about how wonderful she is and how you two belong together."

He grunts with what sounds like disgust, leaning back in his chair. "The woman's gone off her rocker. I'm sorry, Elena, you should never have been put in the middle of this."

"Not your fault my dream job turned into pimping for my boss."

His lips flatten. "I'll have a talk with Raisa. Your pimping days are over."

"No, you can't," I say too quickly, with too much panic in my voice. "I mean, she'll fire me. I need this job."

I clasp my hands on my lap, my fingers twitching restlessly.

"All right," he says. "I won't let on that I know about her ridiculous plot, but I will make sure she understands I will never go back to her. I've told her before, but this time I will leave no doubts about my feelings for her." He lays a hand over mine, stilling my restless fingers. "At least now I understand why you've been so anxious about getting involved with me."

"You're my boss's ex-husband. Of course I'm anxious."

"But you might've gone to dinner with me in spite of that. Am I right?"

I consider my answer for a moment before I say, "Yes."

He gives my hand a quick squeeze. "Knowing Raisa thinks she can get her claws into me again makes you even more anxious, because you worry she'll fire you if she finds out you and I are seeing each other."

"That's right. Now will you give up on the idea of dating me?"

"No. I will not let Raisa bollocks up my life any more than she already has."

"Great." I tear my hands away from his. "I'm your revenge fuck."

"Elena, no." His gaze is so earnest it makes my throat go thick. "Being with you is not how I avenge myself on Raisa. I'm not vengeful at all. She cheated on me, repeatedly, and often with men who worked for her. I stopped loving Raisa a long time ago, because of what she'd done. When I found out about her infidelity, I walked out the door and never looked back."

"But you work for her now."

"As a favor. I may not love her anymore, but I don't want her to suffer either." He braces an elbow on the table and sets his forehead in his raised palm. "Meeting you is the best thing that's ever happened to me. I don't want to walk away from you, but I understand if you need to distance yourself from me."

Do I want that? Is being with Chance worth the risk of losing my job? Maybe I shouldn't want to keep my job, considering what Raisa has pressured me into doing for her. Not that I've enacted her plan yet. But still…

"I need to think about all of this," I say. "Maybe we should keep our distance for the time being."

He keeps his head in his palm while I slap money on the table to cover my part of lunch, grab my purse, and hurry out the door. I don't see any taxis, so I start walking and head for the subway station I'd seen down the street. I'm crossing in front of an alley when Chance catches up to me. He grasps my arm and tows me into the alley, backing me up to a building.

And he kisses me.

It's no sweet and tender kiss, either. He takes possession of my mouth like he's starved for the taste of me, his lips mashed to mine, his tongue hungry and unyielding while his teeth nip at my lower lip. I moan and give in, devouring him as completely as he's devouring me, dissolving into the kiss, reveling in the velvety heat of his tongue and the blustering of his breaths on my skin.

He cages me against the wall with his body, all those muscles crushed against me, flexing as he whisks a hand up and down my side. I thrust my fingers into his hair and wrap my leg around his, all but begging him to take me right here, right now.

A car horn honks, and still I want him.

Chance pulls his head back, breaking the kiss, but keeps his body plastered to mine. He's breathing as roughly as I am. "I want you, Elena. It's more than sex, but I swear I'll go insane if I can't have you again, soon. Why should Raisa drive a wedge between us? We can't let her have that kind of power."

"What can we do? She's my boss and—"

He silences me with his lips, peeling them away from mine so very slowly. "She's abusing her position by ordering you to help her with a personal situation. That means she has no bloody right to play the victim."

I can't speak. The look on his face, the tone of his voice, those things convince me he's not doing this for revenge. He genuinely wants to be with me.

And he feels so good pressed against me.

He feathers his lips over mine. "Have dinner with me, Elena. In my hotel suite."

"What will we do after dinner?"

One side of his mouth kicks up. "I'll leave that to your imagination."

I swallow, but my throat still feels tight. A forbidden affair with my boss's ex-husband? That's not like me at all, but I want this man. Want him like crazy. He's right about Raisa abusing her position, so maybe that gives me a great excuse to take what I want and not feel bad about it.

"Come on," he whispers, his voice so sexy it makes my tummy flutter. "Take a chance."

"You've already used that pun. Try coming up with a new one."

"How about this?" He backs up a step, depriving me of the sensation of his body against mine. "Roll the dice, because Chance will always be on your side."

I can't help smiling. "How can I say no to that?"

"Does that mean yes?"

"Mm-hm." I lunge forward to plant a firm but quick kiss on his lips. "Yes, Chance, I will have dinner with you."

He releases a gusty breath, his shoulders sagging. "Thank you."

It's so cute how relieved he is, but I'm forced to make him a little unhappy. "But we can't do it until Friday. We've got all those cases you need to catch up on, and you need to prepare for depositions and that injunction hearing and—"

Chance raises a hand, nodding and sort of frowning. "Yes, you're right. All of that takes precedence, which is damn irritating. Promise me we will have dinner Friday night."

"I might have to work over the weekend too."

"But we can take one night off." He leans in again, his lips ghosting over mine. "Say you'll be mine Friday night. Please, Elena."

Suddenly, I have trouble catching my breath. With him so close, smelling so good, I can manage only one word. "Yes."

He grins. And then he kisses me again, even hotter and longer than before, leaving me as warm and soft as a caramel candy in the sun. It feels wonderful.

We go back to work, and though I get my job done like I should, my mind keeps creating images of what Friday night might be like.

Chapter Seven

Chance

For the next two days, I have a hell of a time concentrating on work. I get to see Elena even more than I'd hoped, since she's helping me prepare for depositions and all those other things that sounded so important a few days ago but now seem inconsequential. But I'll take any excuse to spend time with her. We have lunch together on Thursday at Elena's favorite spot, where we have waffles, her favorite, and I tease her about eating breakfast for lunch.

I love teasing Elena. And I love that she teases me too.

When Friday finally arrives, I find myself checking the clock—any clock, wherever I am, from the one on my mobile to the one in Times Square—to see if it's time for my date with Elena yet. Tonight, I'll have her in my bed. Finally. I've had her in an elevator, but this will be our first real date and our first time making love in a soft bed with silk sheets.

I know she'll look stunning with her naked body stretched out on that bed.

We don't get to have lunch together. Elena is at the law library again, and she took a lunch with her, in another of those depressingly brown paper bags. I have pizzas delivered to the office for the paralegals and interns, and some of the other attorneys join me in eating with them. Raisa does not.

Twenty minutes after we finish lunch, Elena returns to the office. I hear her lovely voice, though I can't tell what she's saying to her coworkers. I wait a few minutes, to let her settle in at her desk, then I call Elena into my office. While I wait for her, I darken the glass wall between my office and the cubicle farm until it's opaque. No one will think that's odd, since I often darken the glass for privacy. And I need privacy for what I have in mind.

I'm leaning against the window frame when she walks in.

She lowers her sweet arse onto the chair across the desk from me. "What can I help you with? More research?"

"Yes. Very important research." I crook a finger at her. "Come here, Elena."

"Why?"

"Because I asked you to."

Her lips curve into a teasing little smile. "No, you ordered me to. Bossy much?"

"Yes." I wave my arm this time. "Get your edible little arse over here this instant. Is that bossy enough for you?"

Elena sets her notepad on the desk and stands.

"Shut the door," I say.

"Why?"

"I'm sure you can guess why."

She closes the door and comes up to me. "Not at work."

"Then why did you shut the door?" I loop an arm around her waist and pull her closer. "You know what I'm after."

"I have to say we shouldn't, even though I want what you want." She takes my tie between her thumb and forefinger, sliding them up until her fingers meet the knot. "But I thought you wanted to wait until tonight."

"For the main course, yes. But we can have an appetizer right now."

"Appetizer? Mm, I like the sound of that." She drops to her knees in front of me, her face inches from my cock. "I am famished."

This isn't quite what I'd had in mind, but who am I to deny a woman what she wants? "Go on, then."

She unbuttons my trousers and finds the pull on the zipper, takes it between her teeth, and drags the zipper down. Her gaze stays locked on mine, and I can't look away from the sight of her lips peeled back, the little metal pull trapped between her teeth while she tugs it down, down, down. By the time she's done, I'm breathing hard.

And she hasn't even touched me yet.

Elena slips her hand inside my trousers and eases my cock out. It's already hard for her, and the sensation of her soft hands on me steals any breath I might've been trying to suck into my lungs. While she glides her hands up and down my length, I force myself to take slow and steady breaths while I brush hair away from her face and cup her chin.

"You're wonderful, Elena."

"I haven't done anything yet."

"No, I don't mean you're wonderful for this. You are wonderful all the time."

"Thank you." She puckers her lips and gently blows air across the head of my erection. When I shudder, she smiles. "Let me show you how wonderful I can be."

She opens her mouth, as if she's about to take me inside, but instead shoves my trousers and boxer shorts down to my ankles and presses her lips to my inner thigh. With her mouth open, the liquid warmth of her tongue moistens my skin. I brace my hip on the window frame, watching her face while she glides her tongue up my leg, swirling it while she travels higher and higher. Her hair brushes my cock, and I suck in a sharp breath at the sensation of her silky locks on my skin. Just when her mouth comes within millimeters of where I want it, badly, she moves to the other thigh and starts again, lovingly kissing and licking her way up toward my groin.

The vixen darts her tongue out to within a hair's breadth of my cock, then curls it back into her mouth.

"Are you trying to drive me insane?" I ask.

She slides her tongue across her bottom lip, little by little, the movement so slow and sensuous it makes my entire groin tighten. "Wouldn't you just love to die from pleasure? After all, the French call it *la petite mort*, the little death."

Christ, I would love to die that way—but with Elena's body wrapped around me, her silken flesh gripping me over and over in the most decadent massage. The fantasy of it makes my cock jump, and a delicate laugh tumbles from her lips. I love the sound of her laughter. It makes me want to hold her in my arms forever.

She folds her hand around my length and slides it up and down. "Can't wait till I get to see the rest of you. Just seeing this"—She plants a firm, quick kiss on the head of my erection—"makes me want you like crazy. You have the most beautiful dick in the world."

I know it's bollocks, but I don't care. Maybe I don't have the most beautiful cock on earth, but she gave the compliment with total sincerity. And hunger. Lots of hunger. Hearing her speak those words in her hushed, sultry voice… I might die before she finishes and still be the happiest soul in the afterlife. "As much as I'd love to listen to you praise my cock, better get on with it before the phone rings or someone knocks on the door."

"Yes, sir," she purrs, while she reaches behind my balls to run her fingers along the skin there.

No woman has ever touched me in this way, and it feels incredible.

She keeps stroking my length while she laves the head with her tongue, then flicks it over the very center. And she does it again. And again.

I choke on the breath I'd been trying to inhale.

This time, her laughter is throaty and so erotic it makes me throb for her. "Maybe I should stop torturing you."

Her torture is heaven, but even bliss can be too much. I don't need to tell her that—good thing, since I can't speak—because somehow, she senses exactly how much I can take.

Elena opens her mouth and slides those luscious lips over my cock, taking it deep inside.

I groan at the slick heat of her mouth on my skin. But when she laps at my flesh, I sag against the window and let out a long, guttural noise somewhere between a groan and a growl. She makes soft little grunting sounds while she works me with her mouth and her hand, sounding for all the world like she can't get enough of doing this. I thrust a hand into her hair, gripping the windowsill with the other one, and I swear to God my eyes roll back in my head.

"Fuck, Elena," I say, while her ravenous noises grow louder. I can hardly breathe, my chest heavy with the weight of pleasure.

She closes her free hand around one of my balls and massages it with her fingers.

My every muscle goes rigid, the breath is trapped in my lungs, and I can't stop my body from giving in to Elena's demands. I come so hard and fast I swear I see stars and hear the angels singing to welcome me into heaven. I don't die, though. Elena keeps working me until I'm done, and somehow, I find the strength to breathe again. My heart is pounding, and I can't swear I didn't shout or make some sort of loud noise that's unmistakably the sound of a man coming inside the mouth of the most perfect woman on earth.

I stare at Elena, dumbstruck by her. Isn't she the woman who kept telling me not to flirt with her at the office? And now she's done something far more intimate, and she's done it with tenderness and enthusiasm.

She licks her lips so slowly, and with such satisfaction, that I know I'll go hard again any minute if she keeps that up.

I run my thumb over her lips. "You are... I can't think of a word that's good enough to describe you. Passionate, for sure. And surprisingly brazen. You, Elena, are amazing."

"Well, I did keep saying no to you, and you've been so patient. I figured you'd earned a little blow job."

"A *little* blow job?" I grasp her arms, urging her to stand. Then I cradle her face in my hands and kiss her softly. "That was the Mount Everest of blow jobs. The lovers you had before me must've been very happy blokes."

"Sure, they liked it. But they didn't enjoy it anywhere near as much as you do."

"What a crowd of idiots. Any man who doesn't feel like he's halfway to the stars when he's got your mouth on him must be barmy."

"I don't care what other guys think. But I love that you loved it."

"One good turn deserves another." I turn to face the window, with Elena in front of me. "Sit back, relax, and let me send you to the gates of heaven."

"Do you usually get all poetic after an orgasm? I didn't notice it in the elevator that night."

"We were interrupted then. I won't let that happen again."

"Better not, or I might have to throw your phone out the window." She leans her hips against the window frame. "I hope you're not fibbing about showing me heaven, because I'm so turned on I can hardly stand it."

"You won't be disappointed." I kneel before her, slipping my fingers under the hem of her skirt. "I guarantee it."

Someone knocks on the door.

The nasal voice of Marla, one of the paralegals, says, "Elena, are you in there? We need to leave for the law library if you want to get that research done today."

"Fuck," I snarl under my breath.

Elena throws her head back and whimpers, though not in the sexy way I'd planned to make her utter a noise like that. She calls out, "I'm coming."

But dammit, she *isn't*.

She bends down to kiss me. "Sorry, duty calls."

"Forget the law library. I planned to lure you into every dark corner on this floor so I can kiss you and tease you all afternoon."

"Believe me, I'd much rather sneak into dark corners with you." She straightens and smooths her skirt and blouse. "The law library is musty, and the pop in the vending machine is warm. You smell and taste so much better."

With that, she leaves me.

I sit on the floor for five minutes before I get back to work. My mind taunts me with visions of Elena naked, spread out on my bed, writhing and moaning and calling my cock the most beautiful in the world. She is the most beautiful woman I've ever seen or ever will see. She's more than that, though. She's clever, playful, passionate, determined…and all mine tonight.

The second I get to my hotel room, I'm turning off my damn mobile and telling the desk clerk to hold all calls. No one is going to interrupt us. Nothing will get in the way of my plans for Elena. I will worship her body all night.

Chapter Eight

Elena

The elevator rises toward the nineteenth floor, taking me to my secret assignation with the boss's ex-husband. Yep, this is the same elevator in which Chance ravished me a week ago. Why do I keep thinking of him as my boss's ex? He's my… What? Lover sounds kind of sleazy, for some reason. We have to sneak around so Raisa won't find out. Maybe sleazy is the word for it.

Being with Chance doesn't feel sordid. It makes me feel so good in so many ways, despite the fact I promised to help Raisa get him back.

I glance down at my dress to make sure it didn't get wrinkled on the cab ride to the hotel. I had to go home to change clothes. I'm wearing my red dress, the nicest thing I own, the one I bought for an office Christmas party two years ago. The firm I'd worked for then had rented a ballroom for the party and invited everyone to dress up. Chance texted me earlier to say "wear something special," so here I am in my red dress.

The elevator stops. I get out and, following Chance's instructions, turn left and walk to the door at the end of the hall. It has a sign on it that says "Presidential Suite."

I'm going to have sex in a suite at a luxury hotel. For a moment, I just stand there while I let that fact soak into my psyche. Until tonight, the fanciest place I've done the deed was at a Motel 6 in Pittsburgh.

Straightening, rolling my shoulders back, I knock on the door.

It swings open instantly, like he's been standing right on the other side waiting for me.

Warmth rushes through me at the sight of him, and I have the dumbest urge to fan myself with my hand.

Chance is wearing nothing but a towel.

I do raise my hand to fan myself but stop short of my face. Then I wave at him like an idiot to cover the fact I'd been about to fan myself. Honestly, can anyone blame me? He looks hotter than hot in a white towel that seems like it'll fall off at any second. I let my gaze wander over his naked chest, admiring the lines of all those muscles while I imagine running my tongue over every single one of them.

"Good evening, Elena."

When he smiles at me, the seductive slant of his lips makes me want to throw myself at him.

"Uh, hi," I say. *So lame, Elena.* "Guess I'm overdressed. I thought 'special' meant formal, but I guess I should've worn a towel."

"I'd thought to feed you first, but then I realized I can't wait one more second to make love to you." He offers me his hand, and when I take it, he guides me into the room. "You are stunning, Elena. Even more beautiful than when you wear a conservative business suit. I love that tight skirt you wore the other day, but this dress is even better."

"Thank you." I watch him shut the door, unable to tear my focus away from his chest. I know what his dick looks like—and feels like, and tastes like—but seeing all of him makes me so aroused I fight to keep from tearing that towel off. "I love you in a suit, but terrycloth is definitely the sexiest thing I've seen you in."

He whips off the towel, tossing it away.

We are standing in a living room. A large, curved sofa takes up most of the space, with various tables and some chairs arranged around it. I can see a doorway that leads into the bedroom. Floor-to-ceiling windows overlook the city, and the lights of countless buildings and streetlights twinkle like stars, overshadowing the sky. Sliding glass doors open onto a balcony where a table and chairs wait, but we're not going out there.

Chance takes my hand and leads me into the bedroom.

An enormous bed is the centerpiece of the room. A window offers a view of the city, but the semitransparent drapes obscure the vista. Chance turns a dial on the wall beside the door, and the lighting inside the room dims to a sensual glow that seems to burnish his skin, turning him into a golden statue of a sex god.

Damn, he's gorgeous.

I notice the covers are already pulled back on the bed.

He comes up behind me and unties the bow I'd carefully tied earlier, the one that keeps my halter dress from falling down to my waist. He lets the straps go. They slide down my body until all of me from the waist up is bared to him. He slips his fingers inside the fabric and pushes my dress over my hips. It flutters to the floor, a pool of silky scarlet at my feet.

I thank heaven I decided against wearing pantyhose, but I'm even more grateful I had the audacity to ditch the underwear. Waiting for Chance to strip those off might've killed me. His fingers grazing my skin, the soft murmur of his breaths, and the scent of him... All those things have me so turned on I'm not sure I can walk the five feet to the bed. Weak with lust? I've never experienced this before, but I like it.

He scoops me up and carries me to the bed, setting me down on the unbelievably soft sheets. They feel so good against my skin that I want to roll around on them, but I can't move. The vision of him entrances me. Sure, I've seen naked men before. But Chance is not like anyone else. He stands beside the bed, far enough away to grant me a full view of his nude body, and gives me time to absorb the sight.

I drink it all in, every muscle and every bit of flesh, from his strong thighs to his washboard abs and those biceps that are well-defined but not outrageously big. His smooth chest begs to be kissed and licked, but my gaze keeps drifting back to that mouth-watering cock, framed by his lean hips.

He saunters to the bed and climbs onto it, kneeling at my feet. While he explores my body with his gaze, he groans softly. "Elena, you are a work of art."

If anyone else told me that, I'd think it was bullshit. But Chance isn't the kind of man who lays on the phony compliments so thick you need a shovel to dig your way out of it. I know he means it.

I watch him while he keeps exploring me with his gaze, loving the way his lips part and his pupils grow larger. He skims his hands up and down his thighs like he's imagining doing that to me. I want him to touch me so badly the weight of it settles low in my belly and triggers a molten slickness between my thighs.

He lowers onto his hands and knees, his face poised over mine. The blue of his eyes mesmerizes me, and I feel like I'm spiraling down into their shimmering depths, lost in an ocean of desire. He touches his lips to mine, tenderly at first, then with more pressure. When his tongue flicks out to taste my skin, I can't stop myself from opening for him, all but begging him to claim my mouth. He slips inside, oh so slowly, and the sensation of his tongue on mine elicits a soft moan from me.

God, the flavor of him. It's indescribable, and it intoxicates me like no liquor on earth could. I give in to the feel of his tongue coiling around mine, teasing and tempting me with every leisurely swipe, until I'm clutching his arms and making sharp moans that verge on whimpering.

I haven't experienced his body on mine yet. He holds himself up on his arms, hovering over me without touching me.

He breaks the kiss and looks into my eyes.

The intensity of his gaze burns into me, setting my body on fire, a tingling wave of heat that stuns me. I want him so much it almost scares me. But I can't be afraid when I'm with Chance. He's the best combination of everything—safety and risk, lust and tenderness, dirtiness and sweetness.

"Elena," he murmurs, nuzzling my throat. His husky voice weaves my name into a seductive spell.

"Yes," I whisper, raking my fingers through his hair. "Yes, Chance."

We've said almost nothing, but it means everything.

He kisses the corner of my mouth. "I love the way you say my name."

"I love saying it."

A breath rushes out of me when he drags his mouth along my throat, then kisses his way down to my breast. His tongue slides around the nipple, moistening my skin but never touching the stiff, aching peak. I bury my hands in his hair, but still his body lingers above mine, not touching me. I arch my back, desperate to reach him, but I can't quite get there.

He flicks his tongue over my nipple, only once, so swiftly I wonder if I hallucinated the sensation. Then he blows a current of cool air across the peak.

I gasp and arch my back again.

"Elena," he says. "Beautiful, sweet, sexy Elena."

Wetter. Hotter. Hungrier. I need him inside me but can't find my voice to tell him.

He draws my nipple into his mouth and suckles it.

A sharp cry erupts out of me. Helpless to stop myself, I grip his arms and throw my legs around his hips. He grunts but keeps his mouth sealed around my nipple, consuming it like he can't survive without the taste of my flesh on his tongue. Though I buck my hips, struggling to find his erection and take it inside my body, that part of him is still out of my reach. My moans become whimpers that tacitly beg him to take me.

"Not yet," he growls, releasing my nipple.

"Please, Chance."

He crawls backward until his face is above my hips. Staring down at my mound, his eyes narrowed to slits, he utters a single syllable that he draws out into a throaty groan. "Fuck."

I spread my thighs.

Chance mutters something else, something I can't make out, and lowers himself onto his elbows. His face is directly above my sex, and I know I'm so aroused he must smell and see it. He gently separates my folds with two fingers, concentrating on the task like it's the most vital thing he's ever done. With my core exposed to him, he freezes.

The air teases my swollen flesh and the wetness that coats it. I moan for the millionth time, but I don't even care if I sound desperate and pathetic. A coil inside me tightens more and more with everything he does to me.

He shimmies backward a little more, and his head dives between my thighs. Groaning deeply, he glides his tongue up and down my cleft, first on one side, then the other.

I clench the sheets so hard my fingers ache, but other parts of me ache even more.

Up and down he strokes me, over and over until I'm gasping and writhing. He stops suddenly, his face between my legs but his tongue no longer touching me.

"Please," I beg.

He presses his mouth to my taut nub.

"Oh God," I moan as I thrash and lift my hips.

He pulls my clitoris into his mouth and suckles with the same strength and determination he'd applied to my nipple, only this time he's touching the most sensitive part of me. I cry out, my back flattening into the mattress, my entire body wrenching from the power of the climax that barrels through me. I want to scream, but I can't capture enough air to fill my lungs. So instead, I grip his head and ride out the pleasure, my heart pounding and my sex pulsating.

When my release finally subsides, I lay limp on the bed, my chest heaving. I manage to mumble two words. "Oh, Chance."

He raises up on his elbows to look at me. "You taste so good I could do that all night."

I regard him with what must be a dazed expression. Though he's given me the best orgasm ever, I want more. I want all of him.

Chance kisses my belly and rises to crouch over me again. He grabs something out of a drawer in the bedside table. I realize it's a condom when he rips the little packet open. Within seconds, he's rolled it on.

Anticipation sizzles through me, and I can barely breathe. Just two words spill from my lips, those syllables infused with all the longing and lust I've stored up inside me for days.

"Please, Chance."

Chapter Nine

Chance

Elena Linwood is perfect. The moment she shed her cloth-ing, she let go of all her inhibitions and gave in to the pleasure, every moan and every movement evidence of how she abandons herself to the moment. I couldn't watch her come, with my head between her legs, but now I have the chance to do just that. Witness her pleasure. Experience it. Feel it, see it, taste it, drown myself in the way she revels in sex. I got a glimpse of it that night in the eleva-tor. But tonight…

Elena gazes at me with a mesmerized expression, her lips parted and her every breath a whisper of unspoken desire. A faint blush col-ors her cheeks, but she's finally caught her breath. When she smiles, it's slightly crooked and entirely captivating. "Wow, Chance. That was… I mean, I don't know what else to say. You rock."

I chuckle. "Thank you, love. I appreciate the compliment."

"Oh no, that was not a compliment. It was unbridled adora-tion." She reaches out to stroke my cock with her hand. "I'm so ready for the rest."

With all of her laid out beneath me, I sit back on my heels and take a moment to absorb the sight of her nude, aroused body. Her taut nipples jut up, their color darkened to a dusky shade of rose. I skim my hands down her belly, past her perfect little navel, and spread them over her hips. She has the most intoxicating combination of curves and muscles I've ever seen, soft in all the best places but with enough strength to make sex with her an aerobic workout, if I want that. With her clever mind and sense of humor, I have no doubts we could have the most inventive, energizing sex imaginable. And I can imagine many, many creative ways to make her gasp and moan.

Right now, all I want is to touch her—with my hands, my mouth, everything—and then lose myself in the sweet release of making love to her.

I rest my fingertips over her mound and wriggle my fingers to tease the curly hairs. When Elena sucks in a breath, I ease my fingers between her folds. It's like wrapping pure silk around my hand, silk drenched with warm, sweet honey. I know what she tastes like, and I'm hungry for more of her, but I pull my hand away. Time for me to prove to her I can do better than shoving her against an elevator wall. It's only been a week since that first night, but it feels like a lifetime of waiting and wanting her.

"Chance," she murmurs. "Please, I want you so much."

The way she catches her bottom lip with her teeth, it's the sweetest thing I've ever seen, and the most arousing. I straddle her body again and push inside her gradually, letting myself experience every inch of her hot flesh. It closes around me like her mouth had earlier today, only better because now she's wrapping around me completely, her body a glove that encloses my cock. I remember the sensation of her mouth and tongue on my skin, but having all of her molding to my length… The pleasure is indescribable.

She grips my arms, lifting her hips into my thrusts.

I can't look away from her even if I wanted to. The lust in her eyes makes me crave her even more, but there's a tenderness behind the need, and it compels me to take all of her I can take. I lower my body onto hers little by little, waiting to see if my weight is too much. When her lips curve into a satisfied smile and she nods, I press all my weight down on her. God, the feel of her. All that smooth skin against mine, the rigidness of her nipples contrasting with the cushion of her breasts. I brace my arms at either side of her shoulders, my face above her head. The flowery scent of her hair makes me dip my head to draw in a lungful of it. She smells so good, from her hair to the musk of her sex.

I pull my hips back and plunge deep.

"Oh yes," she moans. "I love this."

Christ, I love it too. She's so wet and warm and willing, and I want this feeling of intimacy and desire to stretch on forever, so I can memorize every second of it. She bends her knees, framing my hips with them, and wraps her arms around me, her every breath transformed into a moan or a tender little sound of enjoyment. I bury my face in her hair while my thrusts become faster and more powerful. Her name spills from my lips again and again, the tone of my litany growing harsher the more I say her name. Her neck arches, and she whispers into my ear the words that shatter my self-control.

"Don't hold back. Please, I want all of you, all the way."

I lever up with my arms, pull my hips back until I've almost left her body, and drive into her. Though the pace and strength of my thrusts increases, I still can't tear my gaze away from hers. Even the bouncing of her breasts can't make me break the tether linking our gazes. Her eyes are half closed, her expression the embodiment of desire. I watch in awe as her climax comes over her gradually, first her face tightening and her eyes squeezing shut, then her fingers clenching my arms until the nails dig into my skin, and finally her entire body freezes and her mouth falls open on a frozen breath.

Her slick softness around my cock transforms into pulsing waves of muscle that grip and release me, over and over, while the breath she'd held rushes out of her as a strangled cry. She shouts my name even as her body relaxes for a moment only to tighten again with another wave of rippling spasms that push me over the edge with her. I thrust so hard and deep her body bounces, and I come apart inside her. It's like an electric jolt firing under my skin, making every muscle rigid while I throw my head back and shout.

I collapse on top of her.

She threads her fingers through my hair, peppering light kisses over my throat.

I haul in breath after breath until I've regained some of my wits. Then I withdraw from her body reluctantly—she feels so fucking good—then toss the condom in the bin beside the bed and roll onto my side next to her. Elena still seems dazed, her eyes closed and her breathing heavy.

"Have I done you in?" I ask.

"Mm-mm." She takes a deep breath, exhaling it slowly, and flips onto her stomach. Her elbows raise her head and shoulders as she throws me a sidelong look, her sexy lips curling into a smile of pure satisfaction. "That was fantastic. Elevator sex was hot, but this was beyond better."

"Glad you enjoyed yourself." I skate my palm along the curve of her spine. "You are the most sensual woman I've ever taken to bed."

"So, what now? Dinner? Or more sex?" She tosses her hair in a deliberately saucy way. "I vote for more sex, followed by room service."

"But you wore a sexy frock for me. Don't you want the elegant dinner I promised you?"

"Yeah, but I want more of you first. How late is the restaurant open?"

"Until ten, I think." I run my palm back up her spine and along her shoulder. "I need to tell Raisa I'm seeing someone."

Yes, don't I know exactly how to ruin a mood? As much as I'd rather make love to Elena for hours, we need to talk about how this will work once we get back to, well, work.

Elena springs up into a sitting position, her wide eyes on me. "You can't tell Raisa we're dating. She'll fire me so fast the whole building will spin. I'll never get another job if she tells everyone what a husband-stealing slut I am."

"I won't tell her who I'm dating. But she needs to know I am seeing someone, so she'll give up her ridiculous idea that she and I might reconcile."

"Oh, I'm sure that'll put her in a great mood."

"Relax, we can get through this together." I sit up and frisk my hands up and down her arms. "We're adults, and we don't need permission to have a relationship. Raisa will calm down, eventually."

Elena's head droops, her hair falling over her face. "I'm such a scummy liar. Raisa asked me to help her win you back, and instead I sleep with you."

"She had no right to order you to interfere in her personal life." I cradle Elena's face in my hands, lifting her head so she looks at me. "I want you, Elena, not my ex-wife. I like you, and I want us to get to know each other. That's what dating is, right? It's been a while since I tried it."

"I like you too, Chance. And I want the same thing, but…"

Raisa. My ex-wife is the "but" standing between me and Elena. I need to clear the air with Raisa and make sure she understands there is no chance of reconciliation. I've told her before, many times, but this time she will listen. She has to.

Because I will never give up Elena.

"Let me handle Raisa," I say. "Maybe it was a mistake for me to take the job at her firm. Quitting might be the best way to prove to her I mean it when I say it's over."

"Fabulous idea," Elena says with breezy sarcasm. "That'll put her in a terrific mood. I'll be fired ten seconds after you quit and blacklisted an hour later."

"Raisa isn't vindictive. She's still coming to terms with the divorce, but she will get over it."

"Maybe you should find her a boyfriend, so I don't have to play matchmaker for the two of you."

I cup her face again and kiss her gently. "Don't assume the worst. Let's see how this plays out when I tell Raisa I'm dating someone else."

Elena moans with so much misery that I can't help folding my arms around her. "Trust me. I know Raisa, and she listens to me. I will not let her do anything rash."

She snuggles into me, her cheek on my shoulder, the sweet warmth of her surrounding me. "Okay. I trust you. Do whatever you think is best."

"Thank you." I comb my fingers through her hair, loving the feel of the silky strands on my skin. "Everything will work out, you'll see."

And I pray I won't be making a liar of myself.

Chapter Ten

Elena

The next morning, everything starts out wonderful. I wake up with Chance's body molded to mine, his arm draped over my belly and his breaths fluttering my hair. We both lie on our sides, and his stiffening cock pushes against my backside. I lie there for a few minutes, enjoying the comfort of starting the morning this way and remembering all the pleasure we gave each other last night.

Eventually, Chance wakes up. Before I can even finish saying good morning, he's making love to me. It's the sweetest sleepy sex ever, and the best way to start the morning.

But afterward, I have to disappoint us both. "I need to work today, and tomorrow. Not only do I have stuff to do for you, but Raisa piled on more."

"I should work too, but I'd much rather stay in bed with you."

His sleepy-sexy voice makes me want to curl up with him under the covers and never leave. But we both know what we need to do, so we climb out of bed and take a shower together. Okay, maybe that "shower" involved orgasms. We did get clean too…eventually.

I freak out when I realize I'll be walking into the office wearing a red evening dress that's a rumpled advertisement for the fact I didn't sleep at home last night. My panic seems to amuse Chance.

He smiles and says, "The hotel has a boutique, and there's a clothing store down the street. I'll pay, obviously, since it's my fault your clothes are a mess. I'm the one who tossed your frock on the floor and never bothered to pick it up."

"Even if it wasn't wrinkled, I can't wear an evening dress to work."

"I said I'll buy you whatever you need."

Maybe I should say no to letting him buy me an outfit, but I can't think of any reason not to let him. I need work-appropriate clothes. Sure, I should've thought to bring an outfit for the morning, but I'd expected to leave after dinner and sex. We never made it to the hotel restaurant, though. Chance ordered room service, and we fed each other while naked on the bed. Which probably explains the crumbs stuck to my ass.

Last night was so good I half suspect I dreamed it.

Today might turn into a waking nightmare. Raisa will be at the office for sure.

Way to be positive, Elena.

I pull on my fancy dress and let Chance take me to the hotel boutique. Everything is so expensive I don't feel comfortable buying a new outfit there.

"Go on," Chance says in a tone so seductive I'm ready to do anything he asks. "Splash out this one time."

Yeah, I'll probably do that if I figure out what the heck it means. "I'm not planning to jump in a swimming pool."

He makes a sound that's halfway between a laugh and a sigh. "Splash out means to spend an obscene amount of money on something you don't need."

"But I do need clothes, something I can wear to work without making everybody think I've won the lottery. Please take me to the shop down the street." I raise my hands, palms pressed together in a pleading gesture. "Please, please, please."

"Have it your way."

We head down to the other boutique, which turns out to be middle-of-the-road expensive instead of I'm-married-to-royalty extravagant. I choose an elegant but reasonably priced pantsuit, ignoring Chance's flirtatious comments about how much he loves me in a skirt. I love his smile and his winks whenever he tells me something like that.

We agree to arrive at work separately. Chance goes first, since he always gets there earlier than anyone else except for Raisa. This morning, he's not as early as usual. I amble in twenty minutes later.

Only a handful of my coworkers are there. I briefly wonder if some of those lucky dogs got the weekend off, then realize they're probably off doing research somewhere or writing summaries in their PJs at home.

Chance is already in Raisa's office. I can't see them because the door is closed and the glass has been turned opaque, but I hear their voices. Even when I can't understand the words, I recognize Chance's voice. And I realize, based on their tones, that they're arguing.

Not loud enough to raise eyebrows. Luckily, everyone else is busy and not paying attention to the voices coming from Raisa's office.

I sit down at my desk and try to work, but my gaze keeps gravitating to the door to Raisa's office. How bad is it in there? Is Chance okay? I can't go in there to check without some legitimate excuse.

Grabbing a folder from my desk, I march up to Raisa's office door. Their voices are louder now, but I still can't make out the words. Chance sounds annoyed. Very annoyed.

I hesitate for a couple seconds, then knock.

Everything goes quiet inside the office.

The toe of my brand-new shoe taps furiously while I chew the inside of my lip.

At last, the door swings open.

Chance looks tired, but he moves aside and gestures for me to enter the room.

I can't make my feet budge. "I, um, need to talk to you about that pharmaceuticals case. I have the summaries you asked for, but I want to make sure it's everything you need."

He gives me a grateful look, one Raisa can't see since his back is turned to her. "I'll take a look later, but thank you for checking in with me."

Raisa rises from her chair, shoulders back, chin lifted, her cool gaze trained on me. "You should join us, Elena."

"No," Chance says. "This has nothing to do with her."

She ignores him and speaks to me. "Come in, Elena."

I shuffle into the office, my feet like big rocks attached to my legs with massive iron chains, and take a seat in one of the chairs on this side of Raisa's desk. Chance drops into the other chair. Only a couple feet separate us, but though I long to touch him, I don't do it.

Raisa can't know about us. Not unless Chance told her, and he wouldn't do that. She is one of the top legal minds in the country, a smart woman who can be very perceptive when she wants to be. So far, she's seemed oblivious of the chemistry between me and Chance, but maybe she's set her perceptive mind to the task of figuring out who he's dating.

I assume he's told her that much.

Raisa remains standing, like the teacher about to ream her wayward students. Or student. She's looking straight at me when she says, "I know about you and Chance."

Every ounce of blood in my body seems to evaporate, leaving me cold and stunned. I feel like I might pass out, but that's just crazy. I don't faint because my boss finds out I'm sleeping with her ex-husband. I sit up straighter instead, my hands flat on the folder on my lap.

Chance's gaze flicks to me. "She knows I sweet-talked you into telling me about her little scheme. I've made it clear to Raisa I don't appreciate or approve of the way she bullied you into helping her spy on me."

I can't think of a damn thing to say. Spy on him? I guess he's talking about Raisa's plan to win him back.

Chance aims a squinty-eyed look at Raisa. "I've set her straight on all of that."

Raisa waves a hand in my direction. "Forget about the plan, Elena. I shouldn't have asked you to do that."

"And?" Chance prompts.

She meets my gaze. "I'm sorry for what I did."

Wow, she apologized. Maybe I won't be fired after all.

"I appreciate that," I tell her.

"See?" Raisa says to Chance. "It's all settled."

"Yes, that's a good start." He gets up and nods to me, then to Raisa. "This matter is settled, and I'd better not hear anything more about you trying to win me back."

"Of course not," Raisa says.

Chance casts a furtive glance at me, smiling faintly, then walks out.

"Shut the door," Raisa calls out, and he does it.

I'm alone with my boss. Who just found out her ex is seeing someone else. So yeah, I grasp the arms of my chair while pretending to be relaxed.

Raisa sits down, clasps her hands on the desktop, and eyes me with her lips pinched. Though I've worked for her for barely more than a week, I've come to know that expression. It means she's figuring out whether I've kept something from her. Which I have. Big time. My conscience urges me to confess everything, but even if I wanted to, I can't do that without talking to Chance first.

"I know what you've been doing," Raisa says, leaning back in her chair, still staring at me in a way that makes my skin crawl.

Fighting the urge to scratch my arms, I try to look innocent. Jeez, I was dealing with one of the toughest lawyers in New York, and I thought I could fool her? Well, she hadn't figured out the truth yet. Maybe that snowball wouldn't melt in Hell after all.

"You had a fling last night, didn't you?" Raisa asks. "It's all right. After being at the law library most of the week, I imagine you needed to cut loose for a night. But I need you sharp, Elena, not tired and distracted."

I almost cry from relief. She clearly doesn't know I slept with Chance last night, though she's guessed I spent the night with someone. "I'm fine, really. Only had one martini last night, so no hangover."

"Good, but I'm not talking about hangovers." She waves a finger toward my face. "You have bags under your eyes, and that's a new suit from Sheri Ann's boutique. She's a friend, and I know what she keeps in stock. And the price tag is hanging from your armpit."

Is it? I lift my arm, and yes, the tag is hanging there. Damn. Isn't that just my luck? Raisa knows the woman who owns the boutique where Chance bought me a new outfit. I hope Sheri Ann didn't recognize Chance. I mean, if Raisa bought clothes there...

She's studying me again, like she knows I've done something but can't quite put her finger on it.

"If that's all," I say, "I should get these summaries to Chance."

"Not yet." She swivels her chair side to side. "You've let me down, Elena. I asked you to do one simple thing—find out who Chance is sleeping with—and you failed."

"I'm sorry."

She puckers her lips again, steepling her index fingers under her chin. "Never mind. I'll find out on my own. You're dismissed."

And of course, she waves her hand to indicate I should leave.

I've just shut the door behind me, intending to head for Chance's office, when a strange noise inside Raisa's office makes me stop. I tip my head to the side, listening. It almost sounds like crying. Sniffling, for sure.

Oh God, she's upset. About Chance dating someone else.

Which means her tears are my fault.

Feeling like the slimiest, wartiest toad on the planet, I go to Chance's office and shut the door behind me when I get there. I set the folder on his desk. "She's not giving up. I've been fired from being her little spy, but Raisa says she'll figure out on her own who you're sleeping with."

"She's bluffing. Lawyers are good at that."

"After I closed the door to her office, I heard Raisa crying."

He goes stiff, his unblinking gaze nailed to mine. "Crying?"

I nod.

"Shit." He runs a hand over his mouth. "I can't help that. What am I meant to do? Take her back so she won't feel bad?"

"No, of course not. But maybe we shouldn't—"

He surges up from his chair and slants over the desk to kiss me. His mouth lingers on mine for a moment, a long and blissful moment of feeling his warm lips and tasting a hint of the tea from the mug that sits on his desk. Though he peels his lips away, he doesn't move back. He stays there, an inch from my face, his sapphire eyes gazing into mine, and tucks a lock of hair behind my ear with one finger.

I try again to say something but manage to speak only one syllable. "Chance—"

Then he kisses me again, fervently, pulling back only enough to speak. His lips graze mine. "I'm sorry Raisa is upset, but she made a mess of things when we were married. She doesn't get to play the victim now. I want you in my life, Elena. We're not doing anything wrong."

"The firm's policy says coworkers who start dating have to report it to Raisa. I don't want to tell her, but my damn conscience kicked in this morning."

"We will tell her, once she calms down. The policy gives us thirty days, remember?"

"She seemed pretty damn calm when she told me I'd failed her and that she'll figure out on her own who you're sleeping with."

"And then she cried." He drags the backs of his fingers down my cheek. "I just told her I'm seeing someone. Let her digest that information before we tell her the rest."

It makes sense. But I have an annoying habit of being the good girl who follows the rules to the letter, sometimes going beyond what's required in my zeal to do the right thing. Maybe this once I can *not* be that girl. Waiting until we find out for sure if we really want to date seems like the smart thing to do. What if after a few more days we realize we're not right for each other?

Sorry excuses, I know.

But Chance is kissing me again, and all thoughts zip out of my brain, flying off into the sky.

He steps back and settles onto his chair. "I suppose we should discuss those summaries."

For a second, I can't remember what the hell he's talking about. Then the knowledge surfaces in my hormone-addled brain, and I hand him the folder and sit down.

For the next twenty minutes, we talk about legal summaries.

And I keep thinking about that boutique owner and what she might've seen.

Chapter Eleven

Chance

We survive the weekend, both of us working our arses off because we have a lot of work to do and because it keeps us away from Raisa. Overworking ourselves also stops us from sneaking into the file room to have sex, or sneaking into the restroom to have sex, or— Well, let's just say there are plenty of spots where we could enjoy each other.

But we don't. We behave like professionals.

It's bloody awful.

We survive Monday too, though barely.

Elena agrees to meet me in the hotel restaurant for dinner, claiming she won't get any food unless we eat first and go upstairs after. She might have a point. At lunch, I took her to a different boutique to buy a new dress for our date tonight. I hadn't known Raisa was friends with the owner of the boutique down the street from the hotel. But then, I hadn't been a part of Raisa's life for more than a year. Longer, really. We led separate lives even before the official separation.

I finish putting on my tie and head for the door while fantasizing about how delicious and entirely fuckable Elena will look in the emerald-green dress she'd let me buy for her. I got a glimpse of it when the clerk slipped the dress into a bag, but Elena had refused to let me watch her trying it on.

"You can't come into the fitting room with me," she'd said, smiling and shaking her head. "I have a feeling I won't get the dress on if you're there."

"Are you implying I'll strip it off you the second it touches your skin?"

"Not implying. Saying it." She tapped my chest with one finger. "You will strip me naked in five seconds, tops."

Since I couldn't deny I probably would—all right, definitely would—I had to give in and wander the aisles of women's clothing while I waited.

Now, hours after our shopping trip, I remember all the clothing items in that store and which ones would've looked best on Elena. Anything would look good on her. She has a beautiful body, yes, but also a heart-melting smile that makes her eyes sparkle. I'm hopelessly infatuated with her.

Thinking about seeing her, in a few minutes, I straighten my tie that doesn't need straightening and swing the door open.

Raisa is standing there, her hand raised to knock.

I stifle a curse.

She smiles, like we have a date and she's early. "Chance, darling, I was just coming to see you."

"You know I don't like it when you show up without calling first." I hadn't liked it during our separation, and that was part of the reason I'd taken a job in Chicago. I also don't like it when she calls me darling. "We're not married anymore. Call first next time. I have an appointment to keep."

She doesn't move. "Please, darling, let's talk this through."

"We have nothing to talk about." I push her hand away when she tries to touch my cheek. "We are divorced, Raisa, and I've moved on. You need to do the same."

"But I love you, Chance."

I sigh, my shoulders flagging, and rub my eyes. "It was a mistake to take this job with you. I thought I was helping, but I'm only making things worse. I'm sorry, but I think I should go home."

"No, please, stay."

I hear the elevator doors open and glance down the hall.

Elena steps out into the hallway. When she sees me and Raisa, her eyes widen.

She looks fantastic in that frock.

Before I realize her intention, Raisa throws her arms around my neck and kisses me.

Elena stumbles backward into the elevator, furiously punching a button so many times she might break it.

I grasp Raisa's arms and push her away from me. "Stop this. It's over. I'm sorry you can't accept that, but you need to."

Tears shimmer in Raisa's eyes, but I don't have time to feel bad for her. After what she's done to me in the past, and her idiotic plot to win me back, I feel no obligations to her. Not anymore. I race down the hall to the elevator, reaching it as the doors shut. I get a glimpse of Elena and her stricken expression, then she's gone.

I sprint toward the stairs but stop at the door. Even if I can run down nineteen flights, I'll never get there before the elevator, before Elena leaves.

Raisa finds me standing at the stairwell door, staring at it. "That was your new lover, wasn't it?"

She doesn't sound irritated. Instead, I sense compassion in her voice. I can't help looking at her.

"Whoever she is, you don't need her," Raisa tells me, taking my hand. "Give me another chance. I'll be different this time, better, more what you need."

I know she's not making a pun when she tells me she wants another chance. She honestly believes I might take her back.

"You lost me a long time ago," I say. "It's too late. Move on, Raisa, please."

Her eyes grow large, lending her face an innocence and pain I haven't witnessed since the day I told her I was moving out of our apartment.

Christ, I don't want to hurt her. But this can't go on, Raisa scheming to win me back while I try to romance Elena. Maybe Elena's right, and we should declare our relationship to Raisa. I need to talk to Elena first.

"I'm sorry," I tell her. "I have to go. It's for the best."

And I swear fate is on my side when I run for the elevator and get there at the instant the doors slide open. An older couple exits the car. I hurry inside and punch the button for the lobby.

Half an hour later, after enduring a long taxi ride amid a traffic jam, I finally stand outside the door to Elena's apartment. I pray she's here. Though I'd checked the hotel restaurant and the bar, I hadn't found her there. She must have come home.

I knock.

A moment later, the door opens—and Elena gapes at me.

She's still wearing that dress, the green number with a low neckline, the one that molds to every curve on her body.

"Hi," she says, still seeming surprised and confused.

"May I come in? I want to explain what you saw."

"Raisa was trying to seduce you, right? I figured that one out already." Elena motions for me to enter. "My apartment isn't swanky, like your hotel, but it's comfortable."

"I'm not a snob."

"Yeah, I know." She hunches her shoulders. "Sorry I ran away, but I kind of freaked when I saw Raisa."

"No worries. I finally got the chance to run after a woman."

I walk into the apartment, taking in the small but very puffy sofa and two puffy recliners. Multi-layered white curtains frame the windows, beyond which I catch a glimpse of the Manhattan skyline glittering with lights. This building is far enough away from that view to be relatively affordable. As affordable as anything gets in New York.

Elena is barefoot.

My attention stalls on her dainty toes and the lavender nail polish on them.

She wanders into the kitchen. A bar separates it from the living room.

I follow her while she opens the refrigerator and pulls out a bottle of beer. "Want one?"

"Love one. Thanks." I take the bottle she offers, watching while she grabs one for herself. "Could we sit down? I was on foot for the last two blocks. Traffic was terrible."

She leads me to the sofa and sits down, patting the cushion beside her. "Relax, I know Raisa surprised you with that kiss. It was obvious."

I drop onto the sofa a little too roughly, making it jump. "Sorry, I'm exhausted from the walk."

She sets her beer on the coffee table. "Two blocks wipes you out? How did you ever survive in New York the first time?"

"A talk with Raisa always leaves me exhausted. Besides, I had to give up on the taxi and run to get here."

"Run?" Elena's brows knit together over her adorable nose. "What was the rush?"

"To find you." I take a sip of my beer, then set the bottle on the table. I angle toward her and take her hand in both of mine. "I was afraid you jumped to the wrong conclusion and thought I was reconciling with Raisa. I'm not, by the way."

"Never thought that." She shuts her eyes for a moment, then looks at me again. "I feel horrible. Raisa is clearly still in love with you, and I promised to help her win you back, then I went and slept with you instead."

"She had no right to make you do that for her."

"I know, but she won't give up. This afternoon, I went to the break room to get some coffee, and I saw Raisa there. She didn't see me. She was crying again, Chance. Crying. Raisa."

What am I meant to do about that? I don't want to hurt Raisa, but I've clearly failed to hammer it into her brain that we will never be a couple again. "I don't love her anymore. I want to be with you, Elena, and that unfortunately means I have to hurt Raisa. No way around that."

"Yeah, I know." Elena lays her other hand over mine. "I guess we have to accept that Raisa will be upset. But I really think we need to tell her about us."

"I don't think that's a good idea, not yet. Let's wait and see if this thing between us is really going somewhere."

"No, please, we have to tell her. And if she fires me, oh well. I'm sure they need paralegals in Siberia."

"You don't need to run that far away. Come with me to Chicago."

Elena lays her palm on my cheek. "That's sweet, but we barely know each other."

"We can change that." I turn my face into her palm and kiss it. "Raisa can't fire you for following the firm's rules about co-workers dating. I'm an attorney, Elena. I'll help you sue her for wrongful termination if she does fire you. But first, I'll try again to talk sense into her. It might work."

"Maybe," Elena says, sounding as unconvinced as she looks. "We're taking a risk either way."

"We are. But you should've said you're taking a chance. I'd jump on that offer."

"Oh, but I knew you'd do that." She taps her finger on my lips. "Not giving you any ammunition to use in seducing me."

"Why not? That's why I came here."

She shakes her head. "No, it's not. You came here because Raisa upset you, and you need comforting."

"Do I get some, then?"

"Absolutely." She leans in, her breaths teasing my lips. "How do you like the dress?"

"I love it." I can't disguise the hunger in my voice, because I am starved for her. I feasted on that body two nights ago, but I need more. "Where's the bedroom?"

She hooks a thumb over her shoulder. "Down the hall."

"Too far." I consider the small sofa and calculate whether I can fit on it lying down. The answer is no. "It's either you on my lap here, or both of us on the floor."

Laughing softly, her face alight with joy and lust, she straddles my lap.

I slip my hands under her dress, skating them up her thighs to her arse. "You've got knickers on."

"Mm-hm." Her tongue peeks out between her lips while she focuses on undoing my tie. "Thought it might be fun to let you rip them off."

"It will be. Enormously." I hook my fingers inside her knickers and yank, but they don't rip. I try again, yanking harder, but still can't break the bloody things. "There's a slight problem with your plan. Your underwear seems to be woven from steel fibers."

She laughs again, tossing my tie halfway across the room. It lands on one of the recliners. "Oh come on, Chance. You don't give up that easily, do you?"

I love her this way, uninhibited, laughing, playing with me. She's adorable and beautiful and sweet and sexy. The fact she has a sharp mind behind all that feminine loveliness makes her even more enticing.

And she's right. I don't give up that easily.

Since I can't tear the blasted underwear off her, I pick her up by the waist and lay her down on the sofa beside me. I make quick work of getting rid of those knickers, flinging them across the room so they get caught in a ruffled layer of one of the curtains. The pale-blue lace panties stand out against the white curtains.

"There," I say, setting her on my lap again. "Please continue."

Elena flashes me a naughty smile while she begins unbuttoning my shirt. "It's like Christmas morning, unwrapping you."

The door bursts open.

We both swing our heads around to look at the man who's lugging a huge suitcase into the apartment. Head down, he grunts when he lifts the suitcase to get it over the threshold.

"Hey, Ellie," he says without glancing up. "I know I'm home early. Cancun was—"

The man lifts his head and spots us. His expression goes blank.

Elena leaps off my lap. "Kyle, what are you doing here? Your trip was supposed to be ten days."

"Yeah, but like I was about to say, Cancun was awesome until the hurricane hit." Elena's brother drags his suitcase to the bar. "We got out just in time. I dropped Amelia off at her place."

Elena fusses with her dress, which only makes her look more guilty.

Kyle wanders over to us, stopping at the end of the sofa. His gaze flicks to the blue knickers hanging from the curtain and then narrows on me. But he's squinting at Elena when he says, "Who's the dude making time with my sister on the sofa?"

I get up and offer him my hand. "Chance Dixon. Elena and I work together."

"Uh-huh." Kyle shakes my hand. "How come Ellie didn't mention you to me? We talked and texted since I left for Cancun."

Elena wraps her arm around mine. "Chance and I met after you left. I didn't tell you about him because this is so new, and we're not sure if it'll go anywhere."

"I get it." Kyle's mouth twists into a sarcastic smile. "I leave you alone for a few days, and you hook up with the first British guy you meet. It's cool."

"Are you being snotty, or are you really okay with this? I can't tell."

Kyle laughs. "Come on, Elena, we're all grown-ups here. Do the nasty with whoever you want, as long as it makes you happy."

I wish my ex-wife had the same mature attitude.

Elena hugs her brother. "Thank you, sweetie. I'm glad you're okay with this, because I really like Chance. A lot."

My lips tighten into a smile, and I make no effort to stop it. Elena likes me a lot. My smile broadens. She likes me.

So much for being a mature adult.

"Don't mind me," Kyle says. "I'm gonna drag my stuff into my room and crash. Unpacking can wait till tomorrow."

He does exactly that, hauling his suitcase down the hallway.

Elena and I watch, and I wonder what my odds are for seducing her tonight—with her brother in the apartment.

At the door to his room, Kyle pauses to smirk at us. "Make as much noise as you want. I'm so bushed I'll be dead to the world the second my head hits the pillow." He nods at me. "Nice to meet you, Chance."

"Pleasure meeting you too, Kyle."

He goes into his room and shuts the door.

I turn to Elena. "Where is your room?"

"Right across the hall from Kyle's."

"What are the odds you'll let me fuck you tonight?"

She grins. "One hundred percent, you lucky dog."

The woman I adore dashes down the hallway, waving for me to follow.

And I run after her.

Everything else can wait until tomorrow.

Chapter Twelve

Elena

This time, the morning after a night with Chance is a lot more fun. I don't worry about showing up to work wearing an inappropriately fancy and sexy dress, because we're in my apartment. When I ask Chance if he needs to rush home to change clothes, he says, "I don't give a toss what anyone thinks of my clothes, and besides, I'm living across the street from the office." Okay, fair point. He can rush up to his hotel room to change. And if he's late, I doubt Raisa will care. She wants him back and reaming him for being tardy won't win him over.

After a round of fun wake-up sex, Chance wants to take a shower with me, like we'd done the morning after our big date in his hotel suite. I'm all for repeating that experience, but there's a problem. The shower is only slightly bigger than I am. Kyle barely fits in it by himself, so I know Chance and I have no, um, chance of squeezing in there together. This apartment does not have a tub. Chance is disappointed but agrees that the two of us getting sardined in the shower will only result in a 911 call and an embarrassing use of the Jaws of Life.

We reach a compromise. He stands outside the shower watching me get clean, then I watch him do the same. He's even hotter when he's wet. The water rolls down his body, outlining every muscle and making his hair glisten. When he tips his head back to rinse his hair, running his fingers through it, I get tingly all over. But when he slathers sudsy body wash all over himself, I'm pretty sure he does it slowly on purpose to give me an incredible view of his soapy bod. I want to climb in there and bathe him with my tongue.

I won't fit. Damn.

But post-shower sex is awesome.

When we finally walk into the kitchen, Kyle is already there whipping up pancakes and bacon.

"Morning," he says. "You guys sure take a long time to get showered and dressed. Kinda noisy about it too."

He gives me a smug smile.

I roll my eyes.

Chance and I perch on stools on the other side of the bar from Kyle. I can't resist laying my hand on Chance's thigh and feeling him up. The bar hides what I'm doing from Kyle's view, not that I think he'll care if he sees it. Kyle has wanted me to get a new boyfriend for almost a year, ever since the last one dumped me for a dog groomer. Apparently, wiping poodles' asses is sexier than being a paralegal. Who knew?

I give Chance's thigh a squeeze.

He rests his hand on the back of my stool and leans in to kiss me. It's a sweet kiss, nothing naughty about it. I suppose he's being polite, holding back in front of my brother, but I like the kiss. Sometimes simplicity is the sexiest thing.

Kyle flips a pancake. It sails through the air only to smack down right where it started, only now its cooked side faces up. My brother is an expert pancake flipper, and I've always envied him that talent. I can't flip a burger without it sticking to the griddle.

"Very impressive," Chance tells Kyle. "You're quite the cook, aren't you?"

"Nah." Kyle flips another pancake, since he has four of them on the griddle. "I can do basic stuff like pancakes and fried eggs." He points his spatula at me. "Elena's the real master chef around here."

"Don't listen to a word my brother says," I tell Chance. "He's a massive liar. I'm no better at cooking than he is. Kyle's trying to make you think I'm amazing so you'll be horribly disappointed when I finally cook for you. Little brothers are obnoxious that way."

Chance kisses my cheek. "I doubt Kyle is exaggerating your skills, but I know what younger siblings can be like. I have two of them."

"What? How come you haven't mentioned them before?"

He shrugs. "Never came up in conversation."

"But I told you about Kyle over lunch the other day."

"True." He scratches his jaw, eying me sideways. "I suppose I should've said something then, but I love listening to you talk."

Kyle bursts out with the phoniest guffaw I've ever heard. "Damn, you've got it bad. Don't you, Brit boy?"

I aim an exaggerated scowl at him. "Be nice. Chance is my boyfriend, so don't be obnoxious."

"Boyfriend?" Kyle looks smug again, but his closed-mouth smile is aimed at Chance this time. "If you're dating my sister, that means I get to razz you big time. Know anything about NASCAR?"

"I've heard the term," Chance says, "but that's about all. It's car racing, isn't it?"

"Yep." Kyle grins with wicked glee. "Let me tell you all about it."

Kyle proceeds to recite every moment of the last NASCAR race while Chance pretends to listen when he's really massaging my thigh. I have no doubt he's not hearing a word of Kyle's monologue. My brother doesn't care if nobody's listening. He can babble away about stock car racing for hours.

After that, Chance and I head to the office via taxicab. During the drive, we discuss Raisa.

"I'm thinking we should wait," I say, "before telling her about us. I thought about it a lot while I was dreaming, and I realized you're right. We need to make sure this thing between us is going somewhere before we go public."

"You thought about it while you were dreaming?"

"Uh-huh." I glance at him sideways. "Don't you do that? Work out problems in your dreams?"

"Not really." He lets his head fall back against the seat. "I'm glad you've seen it my way. We only met twelve days ago, after all. It makes sense to get to know each other better before outing ourselves. That would also give Raisa more time to accept she can't win me back."

"So we're agreed? Keep it on the down low for now?"

"Yes."

I realize what he said and have to ask, "You've been keeping track of how many days we've known each other?"

"That's right. Every day with you is worth counting." He kisses me, long and slow and sexy as hell. "Sneaking around could be exciting."

The way he says those words, with his voice a smoky murmur, excites the hell out of me.

I nibble on his lower lip. "How long do you think we need to wait?"

"Two weeks. If I'm not head over heels in love with you by then, it'll never happen."

His statement sounds innocuous, his tone so casual, that I think it must mean something different in British. I stare at him, my pulse suddenly throbbing faster, and wonder if he means what it sounds like he means. Does he think he's falling for me? Or that he might very soon?

I like him a lot, more than I've liked anyone in a long time. But could I fall for him?

Deciding I might be reading too much into what he said, I change the subject. "Tell me about your siblings."

"I have two brothers, both younger. I'll be seeing them—" He shuts his eyes, groaning. "I forgot. I'm flying home next weekend, leaving Friday afternoon."

"Guess it pays to be the boss's ex. You started work last week, and Raisa's letting you take off early next Friday?" I shake my head. "She'd rip me a new one if I asked for ten more minutes on my lunch break."

"I'd planned this trip months ago. When Raisa asked me to work for her temporarily, I said yes with the condition that I don't have to give up my holiday."

"How long will you be gone?" I already feel a little queasy knowing he won't be here for a while.

"The weekend," he says. "Back at work on Monday morning."

I don't know what to say. Not seeing him for a weekend shouldn't upset me, but it does. I'll miss him. We'll have this coming weekend together, so it's dumb for me to wish he'd stay here instead of going home for a few days.

Chance kisses me again, tenderly this time, and only for a second. "Come with me."

"To England? I can't. Raisa won't give me the afternoon off."

"I'll rearrange my plans. We can leave right after work on Friday."

"But—I—" His suggestion has me so off-kilter I can't speak an entire sentence. We hardly know each other, and he wants me to go away with him for the weekend. When I manage to form a sentence, I ask, "Are you inviting me to meet your family?"

"I guess I am."

He sounds as surprised as I feel.

The thrill of knowing he wants to take me home to his family lasts about three seconds. Then I moan miserably. "I can't go. We lowly paralegals must slave away all weekend, you know. I'm sure next weekend will be no different."

He twists his mouth into an annoyed slant and rubs his eyes. "Forgot about that. Can't you get all your work done during the week? I'll help."

"You want to do grunt work? That's my job, not yours."

"Let me pitch in. Please."

"You want me to go with you that badly?"

I expect him to change his mind, but instead he says, "I know it's early in our relationship, but I absolutely do want you to meet my family. My parents and my brothers. If it's too much too soon, say so. I won't be offended if you'd rather not."

For several seconds, I hold perfectly still and consider the question. Do I want to meet his family? He's met mine, but then, my only family is Kyle. Chance has parents and siblings. I assume they all met Raisa, multiple times.

"Does your family like Raisa?" I ask.

He makes a pained face. "They tolerated her. She's brash and sometimes curt, and she never appreciated my family's way. We're not stuffy. We're...outgoing."

Okay, so I won't be compared to Raisa and found lacking. But they might still dislike me for other reasons.

Chance touches my cheek. "If you're worried my family won't like you, relax. They won't be able to keep from falling under your spell."

"That's sweet, but you're sleeping with me. Of course you think I'm awesome."

His mouth twists into a frown, but it smooths out quickly. "That's not why I'm with you, Elena. You're more than a lover to me. I feel more comfortable with you than I ever did with Raisa, or with any other woman." He smiles, almost shyly. "Will you come with me next weekend?"

I think about it for a nanosecond. "Yes, I'd love to."

This time when he kisses me, it's hot enough to steam up the windows of every vehicle on the street and the ones on the shops alongside it. I don't even care that the cabbie sees us.

When we get to the building that houses Raisa Volkov & Associates, Chance sprints across the street and up to his hotel room to change clothes. I head for the office, so it won't be obvious we've been together. I'd rather wait for him, but we need to keep up appearances for two more weeks.

I'm going home with him. To England. To meet his family.

Holy shit.

Chapter Thirteen

Chance

Two weeks with Elena, enjoying her company and getting to know her better. What can I say? I've never had a better two weeks in my life, despite the nagging worry about how Raisa will react when we tell her about our relationship. I try not to dwell on that. I meant it when I told Elena I will sue Raisa for wrongful termination if she fires her. My ex-wife has lost the plot, at least in her personal life. At work, she's as brilliant and determined as ever, the qualities I used to love about her.

Elena has erased all of that. I adore her, like I never did Raisa. Elena is open and sweet, as brilliant as Raisa but without the fierce need to always win. Maybe I shouldn't compare the two women, but I can't help it. Elena has a light inside her I've never seen in any other human being, an inner glow nothing could ever extinguish.

Her legal summaries are perfect. She gathers research and collates it in a way that makes my job easier. She ought to be an attorney, not a paralegal, which I told her only a few days after we met. When I tell her again, ten days into our two weeks, she leans back against the puffy sofa in her apartment and sighs.

"You assume that's what I want," she says.

"Isn't it? You gave up on law school because your mother had passed away and you needed to care for your brother."

"That might have been the reason I didn't go back at the time, but things have changed." She tucks her legs under her, angling her body partway toward me where I sit beside her. "At first, getting paralegal certification was a detour, and I still planned to go to law school someday. But after a while, I realized I like being a paralegal. Lawyers have to go to court and argue with other lawyers and with judges. After watching that stuff for six months, I decided I'll stick to research, writing summaries, interviewing clients, and all the no-courtroom stuff that I love doing."

"You love research? I've never heard a paralegal or a lawyer say that."

She hunches her shoulders. "What can I say? I love it. Using my brain to ferret out the right information is a lot more fun than playing the lawyer game. And it is a game, right? Like chess and poker mushed together."

I laugh, enchanted by her way of describing the legal profession. "Mushed together? Well, I can't deny there's a lot of bluffing and even outright lying involved. That's why I quit my job in Chicago."

"Thought you took a sabbatical."

"Yes, but this morning I submitted my resignation. I've had enough of the underhanded bollocks."

She studies me for a moment, seeming to weigh whether to say something. Finally, she asks, "Are you staying at Raisa's firm permanently?"

"No. I've had enough of her underhanded bollocks too."

"What will you do?"

I run a hand through my hair, not sure how to answer. "That's yet to be decided."

Elena inches closer to me. "I heard a rumor you're stinking rich. Is that true?"

"Who told you that?"

"Office gossip. I haven't asked you about it because gossip is, well, gossip and it wasn't any of my business." She fingers the top button on my shirt. "Now it is."

"The gossip is partly true." I slip my arm around her, tugging her closer. "I'm not filthy rich, but I have enough money to live comfortably without needing to work for quite a while."

"Would it be rude to ask how you got to be wealthy? Was it a big settlement for a client?"

"You're not being rude at all. I've gotten a few sizable settlements for clients, and I have a mate who's a financial adviser. He helped me invest wisely." I glance around the small apartment with its inexpensive furniture, and I suddenly wonder if my financial situation makes her uncomfortable. "My family are what you might call upper middle class, but they're not stinking rich and definitely not uptight snobs."

"I'm looking forward to meeting your parents."

The way she changed the subject makes me think she might be uncomfortable after all. "Does it bother you that I have money?"

She gives me a sweet, if small, smile. "I have money too, just not the gobs and gobs of it you have. My bank account balance is eight hundred and fifty-two dollars and nineteen cents. Does that bother you?"

"No. But that's different."

"Because I'm not rich and you are. I'm supposed to be jealous or disgusted or something. Sorry to disappoint, but I'm none of those things."

"You honestly don't care?"

"About your money? No. I care what kind of person you are." She kisses me, and her eyes are millimeters from mine when she says, "You are a good man, Chance Dixon. That's what matters."

"You are an exceptional woman, Elena Linwood."

"Are you trying to outdo me with your compliment? I said you're a good man, so you have to say I'm exceptional."

I know she's teasing me. Her tone of voice and the twinkle in her eyes tells me as much.

She tickles me under my chin. "You are pretty exceptional too."

How else can I respond to that? I fuck her on the sofa, since Kyle is out with his girlfriend, and marvel at what a lucky bastard I am.

Near the end of our two weeks, the morning of the day when we will leave on our holiday, I wake up with Elena's body half sprawled over me. The covers have slipped off her shoulders and one leg, exposing her creamy skin. I want to wake her with a kiss and make love to her slowly, but we both need to get to the office.

So I wake her with a kiss and stop there.

We've spent most of our nights for the past two weeks in her apartment. I like it here. It's comfortable and feels like a home. My hotel has all the posh amenities, but it lacks warmth. I'll sleep anywhere with Elena, even in a tent in the middle of the Arctic.

Elena and I say goodbye to Kyle, since we'll be heading for the airport directly after work. I've gotten to know Kyle a bit, and I like him. He has a wry sense of humor and clearly loves his sister. I appreciate loyalty. After being married to a woman who thought cheating was acceptable as long as she claimed to still love me, I'm grateful to have met two honest and forthright people like Elena and Kyle Linwood.

We arrive at the office to find Raisa isn't there. One of the other attorneys tells us she called in sick.

Raisa has never taken a sick day in her life.

Elena and I head into my office to discuss her latest research for one of my clients.

We've just sat down when she asks me, "What's going on with Raisa? That woman never takes a day off. I heard that when she had the flu, she wore a mask and came to work anyway. Do you think she's okay?"

"Ted Fan seems to think so. He's the one who talked to Raisa this morning."

"Should you check on her?"

"Raisa is not my responsibility anymore. Whatever's going on with her is not my concern." I realize that sounds insensitive, which isn't what I intended, so I add, "I only mean that it wouldn't be appropriate for me to check on her, considering that she believes I'll go back to her."

"I guess you're right." Elena chews on her lip for a moment, then grabs the phone off my desk. "I'll call her."

"Raisa has made your life hell. You're not obligated to check on her."

"Don't worry, I can handle it." She dials the number and gazes into space while she waits for Raisa to pick up. I can tell when she does, because Elena sits up straighter. "Hi, Raisa, it's Elena. I heard you're sick and wanted to see if there's anything I can do."

I can hear Raisa's sharp voice when she barks something at Elena. How sick can the woman be if she has the energy to be rude to her employee?

"Uh-huh," Elena says. "I'd love to help, but I have plans this evening that I can't cancel. Maybe Sadie can do that for you?"

More sharp words from Raisa. Her voice rattles the speaker.

Elena looks at me, biting her lip so hard it turns white. She shakes her head, hiking up her shoulders.

Like hell she's giving in to Raisa and giving up on our holiday. Maybe Raisa somehow found out about our trip and is pretending to be sick so she can command Elena to stay here. The idea sounds paranoid, but with Raisa you never can tell.

I snatch the phone away from Elena. "What urgent nonsense are you bullying Elena into doing for you? She's my paralegal. You gave her to me for the duration, until you find a replacement for Lucas Miller."

"Chance, darling, it's so good to hear your voice." She coughs, but it sounds fake. "I have a terrible cold, and I need Elena to do a favor for me. There's no need to get snippy about it. You'll have her all day, and after that, she'll help me. I know you're leaving for England straight after work, so this won't inconvenience you."

Oh, the clever, devious woman. She must have found out about me and Elena, somehow, and she's conniving to keep us from going away together.

I hope I'm being paranoid. Pray for it, actually.

Raisa shatters that hope when she says, "I'll be needing Elena's help all weekend. She's the best paralegal I have, you know. I lent her to you as a favor."

"This is bullshit, Raisa."

"Why do you care so much about a paralegal? You've never minded that I make them work evenings and weekends without paying them overtime."

Yes, I have minded. It may be common practice and legally acceptable to not pay paralegals overtime, but I've never agreed with that way of doing things. It's not the issue right now, though.

"Elena has a life," I say, "and you're abusing your position by forcing her to work overtime."

Raisa fakes a sneeze. "I need to take cold medicine and sleep. Tell Elena I'll see her this evening."

She hangs up on me.

I slam the phone into its cradle.

Elena sighs. "It's okay. I'll do what she wants. It's probably too soon for me to meet your parents, anyway. You go, and have fun."

"Fun?" I flop back in my chair so forcefully it slides across the floor. "I won't enjoy a holiday when I know you're wiping Raisa's nose all weekend."

"She's not really sick, you know. I won't need to wipe her nose."

"That's not the point. I won't go anywhere without you."

Elena smiles, but there's a touch of sadness to it. "That's sweet, but I want you to go. I know you've been looking forward to seeing your family, and they must be excited to see you too."

I spring up from my chair, and this time it sails backward to smack into the windowsill. "I am going to sort this Raisa nonsense right now."

"You can't." Elena waves a file folder at me. "We need to go over this research before your appointment with Arvid Klausen at eleven o'clock. After lunch, you're in court for two hearings. If there's time after that, we need to go over the depositions for the Cutler case."

Fuck. I forgot about all of that. The second I realized Raisa was interfering with my weekend with Elena, everything else fled my brain. I've never let work slide, for any reason.

"I'm not going anywhere," I say. "If you can't go, then I'm not going either."

"Weren't you listening a minute ago? I don't want you to give up visiting your family for me."

My parents are excited about my visit, but the thought of going without Elena, of leaving her here to be Raisa's slave… I feel a strange pressure in my chest when I think about it. She's right, though. I can't speak to Raisa today to sort this mess, and I don't want to let my family down either.

"All right," I say, feeling like a condemned man about to eat his final meal. "I'll go. But we will both confront Raisa Monday morning and tell her about us. It's time."

"I agree." Elena hands me the folder. "Now, let's get to work."

I manage to focus on work, but as the hours go by, that pressure gets heavier and heavier.

Chapter Fourteen

Elena

After a weekend of serving Raisa, like a Roman slave girl without the toga, I can't wait to see Chance again. Despite knowing Raisa has been faking her illness—she has a bottle of cold medicine on her living room table but never took the plastic seal off it—I still feel bad for her. Yeah, okay, I'm a sap. She cheated on her husband and ordered me to help her win him back, but she's also a human being. I get the feeling she honestly regrets ruining her marriage and losing Chance.

I also get the sneaking suspicion she knows I'm the one Chance is seeing.

Sunday evening, Raisa frees me from my servitude, at least until tomorrow.

Chance's flight arrives at eight o'clock, an hour from now, and I can't wait until tomorrow to see him. I run across the street to the hotel and sip a margarita at the bar while I wait. When I see him walk through the automatic doors, I jump up and run to him. Okay, I fling my entire body at him.

He catches me, chuckling, and says, "I'm happy to see you too."

"God, I missed you so much."

I kiss him like we haven't seen each other in months, not caring one bit who sees us making out in the lobby. Chance keeps one arm around me while we get in the elevator and head up to the nineteenth floor. He kisses me even more passionately in the elevator, since there's no one around, and I wish he'd take me like he did that first night. He doesn't—at least, not until we get inside his room.

We've barely spoken to each other, but I'm so happy to be with him again that I don't care. Who needs words? Our bodies say everything that matters.

After sex, we lie naked on the bed with no covers over us, entangled in each other's arms.

"How was your trip?" I ask.

"It was good to see my family." He nuzzles my hair. "But I missed you."

"Raisa kept me busy all weekend." I lift my head off his chest to look at him. "I think she knows about us."

"I think so too."

"That means tomorrow is doomsday."

He cups my chin, his blue eyes intent on mine. "Everything will be fine, you'll see."

"You're awfully confident about that. Did you talk to Raisa already?"

"No." He rolls over so I'm under him. "Let's not talk about my ex-wife anymore. There will be plenty of time for that tomorrow. Tonight, I want to make up for lost time, two days' worth of not shagging you."

We make up for lots of missed shagging, and I fall asleep in his arms.

The banging of a fist on the door wakes us both at six a.m.

Chance yanks on a pair of pants, the ones he ditched last night when we both rushed to get naked, and jogs out of the bedroom to answer the door.

I get dressed in a hurry and find Chance in the living room, an envelope crushed in his fist and a paper in his hand. He glances up from reading the paper.

"She's off her rocker," he says. "The bloody woman has completely lost her mind."

"What's happened?"

He looks at the paper again and shakes his head. "The law firm of Raisa Volkov & Associates is no longer paying for my suite, and

I'm to vacate the premises immediately. You and I are both to report to Raisa's office at eight o'clock."

"What? Shit." I spin around, searching for my purse. Where did I leave it? "I have to go home and change, which means I'll be late."

Chance crumples the paper and hurls it across the room. "Stop, Elena. She knows damn well you're here. Don't know how, but she knows. Go down to the hotel boutique and buy something, damn the price tag. I'll dress and pack and meet you there to pay for it."

I do what he says, because I have no frigging idea what else to do. The woman I'd been enslaved to all weekend, even felt sorry for, is sharpening her ax and taking practice swings with it.

By the time I find a skirt suit that fits and doesn't look as outrageously expensive as it is, Chance strides into the boutique and offers up his credit card to pay for it. I get dressed in the fitting room. We say nothing to each other, but his thunderous expression tells me he is not pleased with Raisa.

The hotel concierge, who seems to know Raisa and not like her very much, offers to have Chance's bags sent to my apartment.

We walk into the offices of Raisa Volkov & Associates together.

All eyes gravitate to us. Everyone comes out to watch us go into Raisa's office, even the attorneys who usually stay in their offices with their doors shut.

Chance shuts the door.

He and I take the chairs in front of Raisa's desk.

She sits in her leather executive chair, spine straight and shoulders back, gazing at us with regal assurance.

My mouth has gone dry. My eyes burn because I've stopped blinking.

Raisa folds her hands on the desktop. "You are both fired."

Chance makes a derisive noise. "Come off it, Raisa. You always overreact when you're angry. Once you've calmed down—"

"I am calm, Chance." She nails him with her frigid glare, the one everybody says she reserves for clients who've lied to her. "You've been screwing my paralegal and haven't informed me of your relationship. That's a violation of the firm's policy on dating."

"That's bollocks, and you know it," Chance says. "The policy states employees have thirty days to report their relationship to you."

Raisa rises from her chair, towering over us where we sit. "I said you are fired. And you can be certain"—she swerves her frigid glare to me—"that you won't receive a letter of recommendation from me. In fact, I'll make sure every firm in the city knows about the gold-digging paralegal who stole my husband."

Chance flies out of his chair. "Elena didn't steal me. You destroyed our marriage years ago, and I should've left you then. I tried to make it work, but you couldn't stop fucking other men, could you? I'm finally happy, and you can't stand it."

Raisa remains unruffled, gazing at him like he's one of the plebs and not her ex-husband. "Don't you want to know how I found out about your treachery?"

Chance looks about to explode, so I get up and place myself between the two of them.

"How did you find out?" I ask, though it hardly matters now.

She lifts her nose. "Sheri Ann at the boutique told me you two had been there and looked very cozy. I didn't want to believe it, but then Chance delayed his flight to England so he could leave after work. He hates to take evening flights, what with the five-hour time difference. Still, I wasn't sure until I asked you to deliver those papers to me after hours, and you claimed to have plans."

Chance comes up beside me, scowling at Raisa. "You wouldn't have evicted me from the hotel unless you had ironclad proof."

"I do." She picks up a manila envelope that was lying on her desk and hands it to him. "Did you really think I wouldn't have a contact at the hotel? Desk clerks are woefully underpaid and easy to tempt with a few hundred dollars."

Chance opens the envelope and slides out the contents. It's a single sheet of paper. When he flips it over, I see the paper is a photograph that was clearly produced on a desktop printer, like the one sitting on a table behind Raisa.

The photo is of us. Me and Chance. In the hotel lobby. Kissing passionately.

Raisa points at the door. "Get out. Both of you. Any personal effects you've left here will be sent to you."

Did her voice quiver the teeniest bit? I search her face and realize her lips are trembling too, barely enough to notice. When I glance at the trash can beside her desk, I see a bunch of balled-up tissues inside it.

Maybe her anger is an act, or a cover for the fact she finally understands Chance will never take her back. I hope that's the case, because if it is, she might get over the initial shock and decide not to ruin our lives after all.

Chance stares at her for a moment, then tosses the photo onto her desk, takes my hand, and leads me out of the building. I tell him he can stay at my apartment for as long as he needs, but he says he has "things to take care of" and leaves as soon as he's dropped me off at my place. His bags are waiting by the kitchen bar. The hotel must have sent them over right after we left the suite, and Kyle must've accepted the delivery.

My brother has gone to work, so I'm alone in the apartment.

In a numb haze, I change into sweats and eat ice cream straight from the container while watching soap operas. I've never watched a soap in my life, and I have no idea what's going on in the complicated stories. It doesn't matter. I'm not paying attention to the TV.

Am I really blacklisted?

The only thing I can do is wait for Chance and hope everything works out the way he swore it would last night.

Chapter Fifteen

Chance

When I get back to the office, the one I was fired from by my ex-wife, Raisa has already left for court. Security won't let me into the office, anyway. I walk back to where I parked the car I hired after leaving Elena and sit there trying to figure out what to do next. I need to talk to Raisa, but she might be in court for hours with her latest divorce case. As much as I want to go back to Elena, I'd planned to have everything sorted first.

Since I can't think of anything else, I decide to get started on my plans for the future. I hope my future includes Elena, but I can't be sure of anything today. Elena is kind and compassionate, the sort who never wants to hurt anyone, even the woman who made her work life miserable. I know Elena admires Raisa professionally, but I think on some level she feels sorry for my ex-wife.

It's all my fault. I should never have come back here.

But if I hadn't, I would never have met Elena.

Though I make a few calls, my plans aren't sorted quite yet, and I finally realize I should go back to Elena's apartment. All my things are there, and I need a place to relax—or try to—so I can figure out what the hell I can do to stop Raisa from ruining Elena's career.

The drive from the office seems to take forever.

I have to park two blocks away from Elena's apartment building, and by the time I knock on her door, I'm in need of a lie-down. Two blocks isn't far to walk, but this day has already taken its toll on me. I can't imagine how Elena feels, but at least I'll be here to support her.

She opens the door and throws her arms around me. "I'm so glad you're back."

A relief so intense it makes me feel weak rushes through me. How can I miss Elena so much after ninety minutes away from her? It seems ridiculous, but I did miss her very much. Maybe it's the stress of our confrontation with Raisa, or guilt over not doing what Elena had wanted and telling Raisa about our relationship sooner. Or maybe it's just Elena. Her smile. The way her hair smells. The feel of her body pressed to mine.

"Come on," she says, taking my hand and leading me into the apartment. "You look like you need booze and a comfy sofa."

"I do. But isn't it rather early for a drink?"

"Not today it isn't."

While I take a seat on the sofa, she gets two glasses and a bottle of brandy from the kitchen. Elena pours our drinks and leaves the bottle on the coffee table. I relax into the overstuffed cushions, rest my feet on the table, and lay my arm across the sofa's back. Elena snuggles up under my arm. The tension inside me disintegrates before I even take my first sip of brandy.

After my second sip, I say, "Don't worry about Raisa. I'll talk to her later and convince her not to blacklist you. She's angry. Once she calms down, she'll see reason. Arguing with a judge always makes her feel better, so I'm sure she'll be in a more reasonable mood after court today."

"I hope so." Elena swirls the liquor in her glass, staring down at it, but doesn't drink. "Otherwise, my career is toast. If the legendary Raisa Volkov wants you gone, you'll disappear from the New York legal scene for good."

"She's not the queen of New York law." I set my glass on the table beside the sofa. "If you want to stay in New York, I understand. But there is another option."

"Yeah, I can move to Greenland."

"That won't be necessary." I curl my finger under her chin and urge her to look at me. When her eyes roll up to focus on me, for a moment I can't speak. She's so beautiful, so sweet, so clever and brave and wonderful. "Come work with me, Elena."

She blinks several times, her eyes large. "I don't understand. You're unemployed too."

"I'm going to start my own practice. There's a lovely little town in New Hampshire where the only attorney within fifty miles is retiring. I met that attorney, Garth Leonard, at a conference a few months ago. We got to talking, and he asked if I'd like to take over his practice." I tuck a lock of hair behind her ear. "I spoke to him this morning. He's retiring in two weeks, and I'd like to accept his offer."

"You're moving to New Hampshire?"

I place a gentle kiss on her forehead. "Only if you come with me."

She sits up and gazes out the window, gnawing on her lip.

"This won't be a glamorous law office," I tell her. "It's a quiet little town full of good people who need legal advice but can't pay top dollar for it. Garth Leonard does have a few wealthy clients, but most are average people. If you want a high-powered career, you'll be better off staying in New York. But I'm hoping you might want what I want—a good life, regardless of prestige or social position."

I've known her for not quite a month, but I feel like I understand what she really wants deep down. If I'm wrong, I'll lose her. If I'm right...

"You don't like New York, do you?" she asks, still gazing out the window.

I swallow a mouthful of brandy before I answer. "I don't dislike it. But being with you has made me realize I want a quieter life, like I had with my family before I moved to America and got involved with Raisa."

"If I say no, you'll go to New Hampshire anyway."

"No, of course not. I'll stay with you either way."

She swerves her head to look at me. "You would give up what you want to be with me?"

"Yes, of course." I clasp her hands between mine. "I love you, Elena."

"How can you be sure after such a short time?"

"I trust what I feel." Lifting her hands, I kiss her fingertips. "I needed fourteen months to decide I loved Raisa. After a week with you, I knew what we have is real, more real than anything I found with her. I trust you, I want you, and I love you."

Her lips twitch upward at the corners twice, then she lets the smile take over, lighting her up from the inside out. "I love you too, Chance."

Something like euphoria sweeps through me, and I can't stop myself from dragging her in for a deep, passionate kiss. She tastes like brandy, but she feels like heaven.

When we separate our mouths, I ask, "So which is it, New York or New Hampshire?"

Elena smiles, and the sweetness of it stabs a wonderful pain into my chest. "I grew up in a small town, and I'd love to go to New Hampshire with you."

I grin, and then I carry her into the bedroom and make love to her. We don't leave her bed for two hours. That's when I receive a text message from Raisa asking me to meet her at her apartment. Elena tells me to go and get it over with.

After kissing Elena goodbye for five minutes, I head for Raisa's.

She answers the door still dressed for court, in her favorite black skirt and jacket. "Come in, Chance."

No "darling" this time. And her entire demeanor, from her facial expression to her posture, is somber.

We go into the living room. She sits in the armchair, while I take the sofa.

Raisa stares down at her hands, wringing them like she has something stuck on her skin and can't get it off. "You and Elena must hate me. I've been horrible to you both. I'm sorry."

I can't speak. Raisa Volkov never apologizes. When I open my mouth, about to try to speak, she holds up a hand to silence me.

"Let me talk first," she says, with no trace of her usual haughtiness. "Ever since you filed for divorce, I've convinced myself you would come back to me eventually, that the separation was a phase you needed to go through. When the final decree came through, it was like a sucker punch. I still refused to accept you didn't want me anymore."

"I know."

She rubs her neck, wincing. "When I introduced you to Elena, I knew you were attracted to her. How could you not be? She's very pretty and very intelligent. Still, I didn't think you would actually get involved with her. I've been in denial for weeks, until I couldn't ignore the truth anymore. Paying the hotel desk clerk to spy on you was unforgivable."

"What are you getting at, Raisa? I know all of this already."

She squeezes her eyes shut, sucks in a breath, and looks at me. "You can both have your jobs back, if you want them. I haven't blacklisted Elena, and I never will. In fact, I'll give her a glowing recommendation if she'd rather find a position at another firm."

I watch her for several seconds, unsure whether to trust her change in attitude. "Are you saying you've accepted that I don't love you anymore?"

"Yes. I know it's over between us, and I hope Elena will make you happy. I know I failed at that."

"The problem was that you never really wanted me back. You hate to lose, and for a divorce lawyer to get divorced was too big a loss for you to stand for."

She nods. "I have an appointment with a therapist. Maybe she can help me work out why I could never be satisfied even when I had a good man in my life."

"Your change in attitude is awfully sudden." I probably sound suspicious, and I am.

"I know it seems that way, but this has been coming for a while." She clasps her hands on her lap, swallows visibly, and says, "Everyone at the office heard our argument this morning. Now they look at me like I'm insane, and they've been literally tiptoeing around me. I took a good, hard look at myself today, and I didn't like what I saw."

A clock on a nearby table ticks softly, but the silence between us is deep, the distance vast. We don't really know each other anymore. After more than a year of denial, I believe Raisa has finally accepted the truth.

"I'm glad you've come to your senses," I tell her, "but I won't be coming back to work with you. Neither will Elena. We talked about it earlier and realized we want something else."

A sigh rushes out of Raisa, deflating her posture. "I understand. And I wish you well, Chance. Elena too. She really was the best paralegal I ever hired."

We say goodbye, for the last time, and I rush back to Elena's apartment.

She hugs me so hard I can't breathe, but I don't care. I bury my face in her hair and lift her off the ground. We kiss, then I drag her down onto the sofa and show her exactly how much she means to me, making her come three times right there in the living room. Watching her climaxes roll through her again and again is the most beautiful thing I've ever seen.

When Kyle comes home that evening, we tell him the news.

He grins, slaps me on the arm, and hugs Elena. "That's awesome, Ellie."

She eyes him like she isn't convinced he means that. "Are you sure you're okay with this? I'm moving to another state."

"New Hampshire isn't that far away. I can live in the dorms next semester. It might be fun."

"But you'll be all alone."

He laughs. "Come on, Elena, I'm an adult now. You don't have to take care of me all the time. Besides, I have a girlfriend and bros I'm real tight with. I won't be a poor little orphan boy all alone in the big city."

"Yeah, I know," she says, her eyes tearing up. "But I'll miss you."

"I'll visit you guys, don't worry." He hugs her again. "Go be happy."

Kyle lets go of Elena and pulls me into a quick, rough hug. "You better take care of my sister. If you make her unhappy, I'll have to do something about it."

"Understood."

He slaps my arm again. "Relax, that's the standard brother thing to say. You're cool, and I've never seen Elena smile as much as she does since you showed up."

I've been smiling a lot more too, since the night I first laid eyes on Elena and she recited German numbers to me. Our future is about to unfold, and I don't mind not knowing exactly what might happen. Whatever comes, we'll handle it together.

Once Kyle goes into his bedroom, I pull Elena into my arms. "Count to twelve in German for me."

She smiles and shakes her head. "Oh please, you couldn't have been serious when you said that was cute."

"I didn't say it was cute." I nibble on her earlobe. "I said I loved the way you pronounce the number twelve. Say it again, and I'll give you the sort of kiss that will make you come for me so hard you'll scream."

"A kiss can't do that."

"Sure it can." I flip her onto her back on the sofa, strip off her sweatpants and knickers, and squeeze between her thighs. I admire the rosy flesh in front of me, groaning with hunger when I see how wet she already is for me. "The lips I want to kiss aren't on your mouth."

"Oh, that kind of kiss." She links her hands above her head, shimmying her hips. "*Zwölf.*"

And I kiss her in the most intimate way imaginable.

I can do this every night for the rest of our lives. I can hold her, kiss her, shag her, love her, and so much more. None of this would've happened if I hadn't seen her drop her head onto the hotel bar, looking miserable and adorable at the same time.

When Elena comes, that light she always has inside her explodes like a star going supernova. I want to watch her do that over and over, all night, every night, forever.

"Let's go to bed," I say. "And you can tell me what sort of house you want us to live in."

Epilogue

Elena
Three months later

I lounge on a cushy chaise, on the patio of the beautiful house owned by Chance's family, and watch my brother playing football with three Brits. Chance and his brothers got a kick out of teasing Kyle when they asked if he'd like to join them for a football match. Being American, Kyle assumed they meant the game in which large men wear huge shoulder pads and helmets and they carry an oval ball.

"Do you know how to play?" Reese had asked. He's the youngest brother, and according to Chance, the one who loves to orchestrate practical jokes.

"Yeah," Kyle had said. "I love football. Played it in high school."

"Are you a good kicker?" Dane asked. He's the middle brother and the most reserved one, Chance had told me, though he'd also said Dane enjoys a good joke as much as anybody.

"Oh yeah," Kyle said. "I love a good kickoff."

Chance chimed in to say, "Now remember, there's no getting your kit off until after the final whistle, or you'll be severely penalized. We play by FIFA rules."

"Fee-what?"

"The Fédération Internationale de Football Association," the love of my life said as if my little brother ought to know that already. "How can you be an experienced footballer if you don't know about FIFA?"

"Well… uh…" Kyle shrugged. "I guess you Brits have your own football association and gave it a Frenchy name. In America, we've got the NFL."

Reese grinned. "Does that stand for Nutters and Fucking Losers?"

And that's when I stepped in. They'd had their fun, but my poor brother was looking more confounded every second. The Dixon boys can harass Kyle more later, when we eat lunch and he hears the bizarre British names for the dishes offered to us.

"They're talking about soccer," I said. "Brits call it football."

"Are you serious?" Kyle asked. "These uptight dickwads think soccer is football? That's beyond lame, guys. Pushing a ball around with your feet is a game for girls."

Now, twenty minutes later, the four of them are kicking a ball around like old friends. They all decided to go shirtless for the game, calling it "the British way," though I know they were teasing my brother again with that claim. Kyle has already tackled each of the Dixon boys at least once, twice for Chance. I think my brother enjoys ramming into my fiancé. Chance can handle it. He might be a lawyer, but he's no slouch at athletics. With a body like that, of course he's a fantastic athlete.

He certainly has all the moves in bed.

I watch the guys for a while longer, admiring my hunky soon-to-be-hubby's bod—and, okay, his brothers' bods too. The Dixons are one handsome bunch. Their parents are good-looking too, but not buff. I met them this morning when Chance and I first arrived at the Dixons' home in the countryside, not far from London. William and Claire Dixon had greeted me with enthusiastic hugs. Nobody mentioned Raisa, but Chance's mom had said how happy she was that her son had found such a sweet girl. I took that as an oblique reference to his ex-wife, the antithesis of me.

Claire and William had excused themselves after that so they could make lunch for everyone. The Dixons might live in a big, spiffy old house, but they still do their own cooking. They have a housekeeper to do everything else.

The boys wander back to the patio. They'd left their shirts in a pile on the grass, and each grabs his on the way back to me. All but Reese pull their shirts back on.

Kyle tugs on his shirt while he trots up to me. He winks, then stretches out on the patio on his back, hands linked under his head.

Reese drops onto a chair, holding the soccer ball in both hands and turning it around and around. His shirt is draped over his shoulder.

Dane sits in a chair beside Reese and takes off his glasses to wipe sweat from his forehead with his shirt.

Chance takes the other chaise, next to me, and leans in to kiss me, holding his lips against mine for a blessedly long moment.

"Lucky me," I say when he pulls away. "Surrounded by gorgeous, sweaty Brits."

"Having fun?" he asks.

"Oh yeah. I could get used to this." I glance at his brothers, then smirk at Chance. "I could have my own harem."

"No, you cannot." Chance lifts my left hand to kiss the diamond ring glittering on my third finger. "You're my slave, remember?"

"How could I forget?"

Kyle snorts. "Oh please. Will you two ever get over the slave thing? It was cute in the beginning, but I'm about ready to report Chance to the cops for running a sex trafficking ring."

Yeah, ever since Chance and I got engaged, Kyle has relished every opportunity to torment us with sarcasm.

Chance's brothers are no better.

"Where can I get my own slave?" Reese asks, still turning the ball in his hands. "I've asked for volunteers, but oddly, nobody wants to sign on for the job. How did you ever convince Elena to serve you?"

"She doesn't serve him," Dane says. "She services him, like an old car that needs constant maintenance."

"And plenty of lubrication," Reese adds with a sly grin and a wink.

"That's enough," Chance says. "You've harassed the Americans enough. Give them at least an hour to recover before you start in again."

Looking at Chance, who's sweaty and smeared with dirt, I can't resist. I have to say, "You need a shower, honey. Your personal mechanic insists on it."

"Give him a good wash and wax, Elena," Rees says, tossing the ball onto the lawn. "I need some maintenance too."

I lay my hand on Chance's thigh. "Sorry, I only service one vehicle."

"Enough car jokes," Chance says. He gets up and offers me his hand. "Let's go, love. I'm feeling filthy."

I let him lead me into the house and to the bathroom. Within thirty seconds, we're both naked. I thank heaven the Dixons have a large bathroom with a shower plenty big enough for me and my honey.

He grabs a bar of soap. "You first."

Chance and I have showered together many times, since we moved to a house in New Hampshire that has a generous-size shower. We've got our law practice there too. Sure, I'm the lowly paralegal in the eyes of most people. But Chance and I are partners in every way that counts—at work, at home, and in our hearts.

A few months ago, in a hotel bar, I'd been offered one hot Chance and taken it. I will never regret that. And yeah, that pun is intentional.

During lunch, we all talk about the wedding. It's in two weeks, and we're having it in America so Chance's family can see our home in New Hampshire. They've never been to America before, since Chance always flew to England to see them—because Raisa hadn't wanted to entertain guests. I'm looking forward to hosting the Dixons, and our house is plenty big enough to hold Chance's parents and brothers along with Kyle and his girlfriend, not to mention our friends.

When I explain about the guest rooms in our house, Reese says, "You used to live in New York City, didn't you? That's where you met Chance."

"Yes, I shared an apartment with the most annoying roommate ever," I reply, flashing Kyle a sarcastic grin. "That would be my darling brother."

Kyle points his fork at me. "Watch it, sister. I know what you and Chance used to do on the living room sofa."

I expect Reese to make an off-color joke, but instead he says, "I'd love to see New York."

The conversation moves on to other wedding-related topics.

Later, Reese corners me and Chance in the sitting room.

"About your apartment," he says to me. "Have you given it up? Or rented it to someone else?"

"No, I haven't sublet it or given it up. Kyle might want to live there over the summer, before he goes back to the dorm in the fall."

Reese studies both me and Chance for several seconds, then he asks, "Could I stay there?"

"At my apartment?" I glance at my fiancé, but Chance simply shrugs. He's leaving the decision up to me. I tell Reese, "Sure, I guess you can do that. We left all the furniture there, so it'll be kind of like a cozy hotel."

"You mean it?" Reese asks. "I can stay there?"

"It's all yours."

"Brilliant!" he says, grinning, his eyes alight with excitement. "Imagine all the girls I can meet there."

Oh boy, those New York ladies are in for it. When Reese Dixon lands in America, every unmarried woman better hold on to her panties. He'll melt them with one wicked smile.

Chance certainly had that effect on me. And he still does, every day.

Reese trots out of the room shouting, "Dane! Guess what? I'm going to shag a New York girl just like Chance did."

Chance arches one brow at me. "Do you have any idea what you've done?"

"Probably not."

Heaven help those New York girls.

Love the

Hot Brits

series?

Visit

AnnaDurand.com

to subscribe to her newsletter
for updates on forthcoming books in this series
&
to receive a free gift for signing up!

Anna Durand loves romance, men in kilts, and cheesecake. Not always in that order. She slaves away every day writing about sexy people doing sexy things together, with heart and humor and sometimes with suspense. With paranormal stories, she explores the darker side of romance. With contemporary romance, she delves into the emotional side of love and sensuality.

Readers and reviewers have blessed Anna's books with wonderful reviews, giving her a nice glowy feeling that she's doing something right. Her books have become bestsellers on every major retail site, hitting #1 multiple times. The Hot Scots series remains Anna's personal favorite and a favorite among her fans. Who can resist a hunky Scotsman?

Anna also has a master's degree in library science, so naturally, she made Calli in Wicked in a Kilt a librarian too. For twelve years and counting, Anna has run a cataloging services company that creates cataloging-in-publication data for other authors and publishers. And when she's not doing that or writing, you'll find her binging on audiobooks, playing with puppies, or crafting handmade jewelry.